Wondrous and Perilous™ Adventures

The Lost Cannon

Adam Dreece

For old-school style fantasy role playing games
B/X, 1e, 2e

CREDITS

Writer: Adam Dreece, **Editor**: Miguel Bybee and Jess Alter **Cover Art:** Joel Docil
Interior Images & Illustrations: Joey Docil, Ken Boledo, Jessica Lamb Gabe Fua, Houmi Art - Anh Nguyen, iStockPhoto.com /enviromantic /DavidGoh, Rick Hershey - Empty Room Studios, Publisher's Choice Quality Stock Art © Rick Hersey / Fat Goblin Games –used with permission **Map:**Megan Beaudoin

Play testers: Lloyd Worth, Tayler Fitzsimmons, Jeff Miranda, Elena Truelove, Anna Cole, Matthew Burnside, Gene Merideth

COPYRIGHT

TABLE OF CONTENTS

About this Adventure

Welcome to the *Wondrous & Perilous*™ *Adventure - The Lost Cannon*. It is designed for 4 to 6 characters of levels 5 to 7 and should take a few gaming sessions to get through.

What you need to play

This adventure requires an old-school gaming system like Old-School Essentials, Castles and Crusaders, OSRIC, Basic Fantasy, or a similar B/X, 1e, or 2e system. *The Lost Cannon* is not a stand-alone book.

For simplicity, the book uses the term Game Master (GM) rather than any other term, like referee, to refer to the person running the game (that crazy, marvelous, story-weaver of a person).

Suggestions and the GM's call

For those that need it to be said, here it is: The decision of whether or not an item, creature, or character has a certain power or spell, how that works, their AC or HP, etc. as written in here are entirely the GM's call.

Everything in this adventure is a suggestion and is not intended to detract from the story, to impede the flow of play, or to make anyone regret committing their valuable time.

Being a GM is like having homework in creative writing mixed with accounting for the purpose of delivering a live presentation to hecklers who are hopefully on their side. I have mad respect for anyone up for running a game, so it (all of it) is always their final call in my books.

Checks, Stat Blocks, and More

If you're not yet familiar with ability checks or with creature stat blocks (aka statistic blocks), or would like a review them, then go to the section at the back of the adventure called *Checks, Stats, and More*.

Creatures

While each encounter area has a creature's stat block and lists what their abilities are, the details for those abilities, as well as other potential details, are found in the section at the back of the adventure called *Creatures*.

Magical Items

This adventure also includes some new magical items with details provided at the back of the adventure called *Magical Items*. If a magical item is to be found there, it has a (See *Magical Items*) beside it when listed.

Otherwise, the item should be found in the standard treasure book, such as the *Old-School Essentials Advanced Referee's Guide or the Old-School Essentials Basic Treasures* book.

Hook

The party has been detained, accused of being members of the notorious Pirate Vocini's crew. Vocini has been terrorizing the peninsula nation of Korusk for two months, raiding its coastal towns and old ruins in search of something.

Vocini is hunting for a *Cannon of the Blessed*, one of four legendary weapons used by the Pirate Queen McFinly of old. It's a powerful-enough weapon to allow Vocini to rise to the status of Pirate King of Korusk.

The capital city's grand magistrate, having learned of the party's arrest, offers the adventurers an opportunity to do more than simply earn their freedom.

While Vocini travels around the vast peninsula in his damaged warship, the party crosses over land to a haunted outpost where the cannon is rumored to lay hidden in pieces. The party's is to find and assemble the cannon, wait for Vocini's ship to arrive, and then sink it, putting an end to his reign of coastal terror.

If the party succeeds, they will be praised and rewarded. If they fail, bounties will be placed upon their heads and sent out by courier ships to neighboring lands.

GM Background

Structure of the Adventure

This adventure has four parts, or acts:

1. Getting ready and heading to the outpost
2. Exploring the abandoned outpost
3. Vocini approaching
4. Pirate landfall

PART 1 - GETTING READY AND HEADING OUT

This is a preamble, allowing the party to resupply in the city and then head out to the outpost by coach. The intent is two hours of in-game time.

The party is escorted by a hero and elite guards to keep the pressure on.

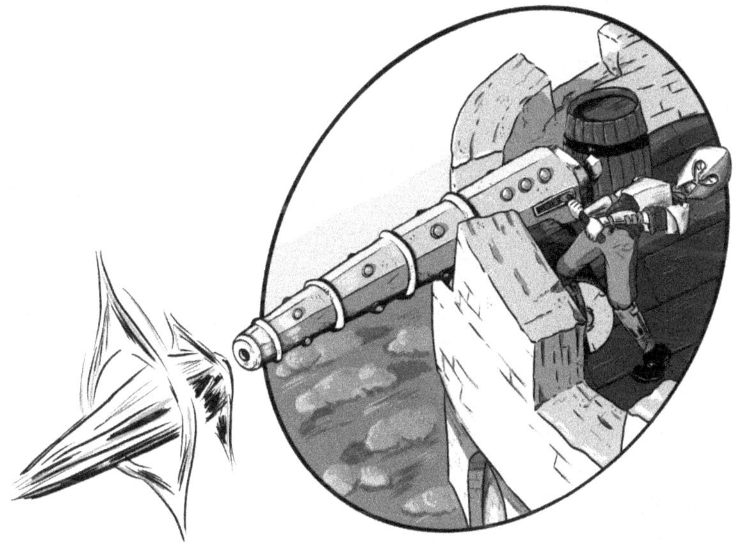

PART 2 - EXPLORING THE ABANDONED OUTPOST

The party arrives at the outpost.

Over the next few hours, the players will explore and search for parts of the *Cannon of the Blessed*. The cannon is comprised of four parts:

- *Barrel.* This goes from the firing end up to the reinforcement ring closest to the far end. In the image above, the barrel is the long cylinder with three reinforcing bands, each one with a single bolt.

- *Firing Mechanism.* This covers from the barrel to the knob, including the part with the firing lever. This is also known as the cascabel of the cannon.

- *Cart.* The *Cannon of the Blessed* has a wheeled cart that magically balances the cannon and attaches to the firing mechanism.

- *Cannon Sight.* This is given to the party at the start of the adventure.

PART 3 - VOCINI APPROACHING

After 3-4 hours of game play, or whenever it fits to heighten the tension, Vocini's ship pierces the fog at the edge of the horizon and starts approaching. The ship is coming in on an angle allowing it to have cannons able to fire when it is close enough.

After another hour of game play, the ship is at 1000 feet offshore (medium range for its cannons, -2 to hit). Pirates onboard will scour the shores with spyglasses looking for potential threats. Every 10 minutes, Vocini's Pirates have a 2-in-6 chance of noticing any party member who is outside and requesting cannons fire upon them. Treat the cannons as if they are a 1st level fighter when attacking the players. If they hit, the target takes 4d6 damage. If they miss but hit AC 10, then everyone within 10 feet of the target takes 2d6 damage. The ship only fires one cannon every 5 rounds and has six cannons per side.

PART 4 - PIRATE LANDFALL

After 30-60 more minutes, or when the party arrives at the tower with the assembled cannon, Vocini's ship drops anchor and remains at 300 feet off shore for ten minutes. This is the party's best opportunity to sink the ship and avoid having to deal with the pirates themselves.

After those ten minutes, Vocini's two onboard mages use the ship's *Staves of Travel* (see *Magical Items*) to open portals for the pirates to make landfall in Area 7 and Area 10. If the ship is hit by the *Cannon of the Blessed* while the portals are open, the mages close the portals for 1d4 rounds before reopening them.

Every round the portals are open, three Basic Pirates and two Tough Pirates arrive in Area 7 and in Area 10. If the pirates are unaware of the party (no firing of the cannon, no one visible on the shoreline), then the landed pirates move to secure Area 4, Area 6, and the tower. After 10 rounds of pirates making landfall, Vocini joins them and they hunt for the *Cannon of the Blessed*.

If the pirates are aware of the party, then the pirates rush the party, potentially moving the location of the portals. In this scenario, the pirates continue landfall for 15 rounds (instead of 10), after which Vocini joins them with a pirate mage to finish the battle with the party.

The ship itself has an AC 4 [15] and 40 HP. It is immune to normal attacks and first-level spells. Up to fourth-level spells only do half damage against the ship. Attacks from the *Cannon of the Blessed*, other cannons, and very large weapons do full damage.

Details on Vocini, his ship, and his crew are in the *Creatures* section at the end of the adventure. Some of the information above is repeated there for convenience.

State of the Nation

The peninsula nation of Korusk is an influential country in the region. A trading and fishing nation, Korusk was once a land of feuding city-states and overrun with giants and monsters.

Two hundred years ago, the great Pirate Queen McFinly unified the city-states under her banner. Then, gathering the best heroes of the land, and armed with cannons and land-ships, she pushed inward ridding the land of monsters and sowing peace with the mountain giant clans. Before her passing, she established a parliament of the powerful families and legislated that a chancellor would be chosen every ten years to rule.

The current chancellor, Nelorin of the Dagmin family, is under tremendous pressure as fighting has broken out between three powerful families, each one seeking to win the chancellorship in the upcoming election. Some believe one family seeks to dissolve parliament permanently and rule as a king while some believe one of the families is secretly in league with Vocini. The truth is a matter for another day. Vocini's raids up and down the coast have been adding fuel to the fire. What is needed, is helping the chancellor deal with Vocini and return the nation to stability and harmony.

A few months ago, it was discovered that one of McFinly's journals from the national archives was stolen, likely part of Vocini's hunt for the *Cannon of the Blessed*. Shortly after, Vocini started targeting old coastal ruins and towns, engaging the Korusk Navy only where needed.

Rumors abound as to Vocini's motivations, some thinking he wishes to lay claim to McFinly's bloodline and, with the cannon, take up the mantle of Pirate King.

McFinly, the Outpost, and the Cannon

Toward the very end of McFinly's reign, a traitorous crew kidnapped her closest friend and advisor, known now only as "The Sea Witch", and stole the last known *Cannon of the Blessed*.

The crew, in alliance with the guards at an outpost, held the Sea Witch and cannon for ransom. Their plan was simple— with the ransom, they would sail away and live like princes. Unfortunately, their plans quickly soured.

Rather than pay, McFinly sent spies to find the hideout of the traitors. This only made the crew and outpost guards become more anxious and daring, changing their demands on a nearly daily basis. Then, with McFinly on her death bed, the base of the traitors was located and a force was sent in to retrieve her friend and cannon. They were soundly defeated by McFinly's own cannon.

After a week of silence, the news arrived of McFinly's passing, wrapped in conspiracies of poison and the selection of a questionable first chancellor. The traitors were uncertain of what to do next, deciding to drink heavily and figure it out later. After some time, and to try to keep the crew and guards united, they offered to negotiate the sale of the cannon to the new chancellor. This earned them more raids on their outpost, which again, they repelled successfully.

One night, one of the frustrated crew, in a drunken stupor, decided to descend into the underground prison to taunt the chained Sea Witch with the grim news of McFinly's death— something they had wisely kept from her. Struck with profound grief and rage, the Sea Witch cursed the entire area. Immediately a haunted swamp took over, and strange undead creatures arose.

It's unclear what happened to the original crew and the guards, but what is known is none who have ventured to the abandoned outpost have returned. Knowledge of where it was and its stories fell out of memory, until yesterday.

Yesterday

Yesterday, Vocini was ambushed by the Korusk Navy. Though he managed to escape, his warship was badly damaged. In the battle, one of his crew was captured and has revealed where Vocini was heading and what he was after: A legendary cannon of Pirate Queen McFinly, known as the *Cannon of the Blessed* (see *Magical Items*). On him was a map showing the location of an abandoned outpost on the other side of the peninsula.

The scholars at the national archive were able to find some notes from the time which indicated that a cannon, in pieces, had been hidden in such a location long ago. They also found a cannon sight said to have been made by McFinly for her *Cannons of the Blessed.*

The discovery of a capable party of adventures having been arrested couldn't have come at a better time.

With violence erupting in the streets between those loyal to the three families vying for power, and with Vocini on his way to the outpost, time is of the essence.

About the Swamp

The main buildings of the outpost are in a sunken area now consumed by the Sea Witch's swamp. The tower sits up on a plateau. The swamp water itself is a thick, green-grey liquid with a sharp, putrid smell that burns the eyes and nose.

MOVEMENT IS HAMPERED

The swamp is twelve inches deep, causing party members to move slowly unless they have magic to assist them. Small-sized characters' movement rates are reduced by 50%, and medium-sized ones are reduced by 25%.

Any character who tries to run needs to perform a successful dexterity check or slip and fall (1d4 damage and prone for 1 round).

PURIFYING THE WATER

If a character casts a *Purify Food & Water* spell on the swamp, it will temporarily create an area 3 feet by 3 feet of clear water for one minute before it becomes putrid again.

RANDOM ENCOUNTERS

After 30 minutes of inactivity, or whenever the players have been deliberating for too long, the GM is encouraged to roll for a random encounter to turn up the heat and eat up precious time.

The swamp-dwelling creature details are available in the *Creatures* section of the adventure.

Roll d10	Encounter
1-4	*Nothing*
5-6	*1d4 Swamp Wight rise out of the swamp silently and attack!*
7-8	*1-2 Swamp Zomtrees rise out of the swamp and attacks!*
9	*1-2 Large Crocodiles leap out of the swamp and attacks!*
10	*A Giant Swamp Zomtree rises out of the swamp and attacks!*

THIN FOG

A thin fog rises several feet off the swamp, providing a layer of magical residue that affects what players see. Swamp creatures are invisible by the fog until they are within 90'. Buildings, natural trees, and general scenery are able to be seen normally. The fog blinds infravision, and similar abilities, beyond 90'.

ZOMTREES AND SWAMP WIGHTS

The inhabitants of the abandoned outpost are a mix of swamp variety of vegetation and undead known as Zomtrees (zombie trees) and Swamp Wights. These creatures are unaffected by silver but are affected by copper-coated, and bronze-coated, weapons as well as by holy water. They are also affected by any magical item or spell that affects plants or undead. A successful *Turn Undead* against them only results in them having a -2 to hit and a -2 to AC for 1d4 rounds instead of making them flee or destroying them.

Swamp Zomtrees are able to make themselves look like withered, smaller trees, transforming back to their regular selves when they attack.

Details about Swamp Zomtrees and Swamp Wights are available in the *Creatures* section at the back of the adventure.

Setting the Stage

Create a narrative for the players with the following points, or read the points allowed:

- The local constabulary, led by a former hero of some renown, Yokik Swiftblade, have been arresting anyone out of place. Suspicions of Vocini's agents or troublemakers for one of the three warring families runs high.

- Yokik, herself, was among those that surprised and detained the party who were traveling without permits. She promised a quick audience with the grand magistrate of the capital city, and within hours, provided one.

- Realizing the capable band of adventurers before him, the grand magistrate offered the party an opportunity to help the nation, earn some reward, and get out of prison immediately.

- The party is to be taken to an abandoned, haunted outpost were the parts of the legendary cannon are said to be hidden. They are to find them, assemble the cannon, and sink Vocini's ship when he arrives. The party will have several hours head start.

- Yokik mentions that if Vocini and his pirates are allowed to make landfall, the odds will shift very much against the party.

- The reward offered for defeating Vocini and delivering the cannon is 20,000gp per member of the party, the right to keep any items found, a small plot of land on the peninsula, and an annual income to support 4 servants on the land. There's is also the promise of a magical item from the great vault of Korusk.

- The grand magistrate makes it clear that should the party fail or abandon the mission, they will be wanted criminals with warrants for their deaths sent to neighboring nations.

While preparations are being made for coaches and horses, the party is able to resupply in town (two in-game hours) and hurried along by Yokik and elite guards.

Rumors

The party has heard 1d4+1 rumors over the past few days.

1. The fresh water that runs through the outpost, it's strangely deep and slippery. Best be careful. (T)

2. There are strange swamp zombies and undead trees at the outpost. (T)

3. There are unnatural creatures in that ruin who fear not silver but are vulnerable to a copper-coated blade. (T)

4. Vocini will offer a fortune to anyone who gives him the cannon. (F)

5. There is a powerful magical item that fell from the sky and into a giant nest of some sort. (T)

6. Don't use the legendary cannon like a normal cannon! You have to turn it around as the barrel draws in magical energy. Also, it must be commanded by a spellcaster whose magical energy it will turn into fiery blasts. (F)

7. The best shot at the coast is not from the third floor of the outpost tower, but the second floor. (T)

8. Vocini's not heading to the outpost, he's headed back to rest. He was wounded in the battle with the navy. The only reason the magistrate wants someone to think Vocini's coming is so that they don't have time to heal. Go in, battle the monsters there, and return with the cannon— weakened and easily subdued. (F)

9. They say the Sea Witch is still alive, still feeding the swamp with her power. If you find her and free her, the swamp creatures will turn to your side. (T)

10. There's been two other parties sent to retrieve the cannon just in the past month. It's a lie that its whereabouts were suddenly confirmed. (F)

11. Yokik is Vocini's sister, both of them secretly fighting to become the chancellor and take over the nation. (F)

12. Don't trust the potions from Drin Kup. He's notorious for getting labels mixed up, especially the cures and the poisons.(F)

13. The magistrate plans on taking the cannon for himself, killing any foolish enough to give it to him. (F)

14. The Pirate Vocini plans to blast the tower once it is in range, just in case anyone's there. Vocini is paranoid. (F)

15. The *Cannon of the Blessed* can only be assembled by one of dull wit and slow mind, otherwise it causes madness. (F)

16. There was a caravan that went to negotiate for the cannon right after McFinly died. They never came back. (T)

17. A renowned hero was having an epic aerial battle above the area a year ago and lost a precious magical item in the area. (T)

18. There's a were-crocodile that lives in the old outpost. (F)

19. The capital city's grand magistrate is plotting to overthrow the chancellor and the whole country. He's looking for a powerful magical item that will let him do it. (F)

20. There's a smuggler's underground lair beneath one of the buildings. (T)

Some time in town

In order not to slow down the adventure, time spent in the city is simplified to dealing with a few merchants and an optional quick stop in at the tavern to collect additional rumors, hire help, or buy rations. Yokik Swiftblade and 5 Elite Guards escort the party to make sure they don't wander off or take too much time (see *Creatures* for details).

Alchemist - Drin Kup

There's a well-regarded, and very well protected, alchemist in town who has good wares to offer. Drin is extremely loyal to his country and refuses to serve anyone who even jokingly says something bad about it. There are always several armed customers around who will protect Drin if needed.

Unfortunately for the party, Drin is low on stock due to his suppliers' fear of Vocini.

- 10 *Potions of Cure Light Wounds* (1d6+1) for 500gp each
- 6 *Potions of Cure Serious Wounds* (2d6+2) for 800gp each
- 2 *Potions of Mighty Strength* (see *Magical Items*) for 600gp each
- 2 *Potions of Graceful Step* (see *Magical Items*) for 750gp each
- 4 *Potions of Cure Poison* for 500gp each
- 6 *Vials of Holy Water* for 50gp each

Bows and Arrows - Bow Fletcher

It's no surprise that Bow is a grumpy sort and has little patience for those who would make fun of his name. He is the best maker of projectile weapons on the peninsula. Similar to Drin Kup, he is low on stock but still has some good wares.

- 1 *Bow +1, +2 against plants* for 4000gp
- 20 *Arrows of the Melee Master +1* (see *Magical Items*) for 30gp each
- 30 *Arrows +1* for sold together for 400gp
- 20 silver-tipped arrows for 4gp each
- 20 copper-tipped arrows for 2gp each
- 20 *Crossbow Bolts +2* sold together for 300gp

Weapons Smith - Ann Vil

Ann is a barrel of laughs for most people. She believes you can only trust those you can exchange trade jibes and barbs with, and that the overly serious have something to hide.

She's a good judge of character. If she senses someone's trying to steal from her or screw her over, she'll kick everyone out and refuse to sell them anything.

Ann's known to have a keen eye, steady hand, and pure talent for making decorative and effective weapons. On occasion, she'll make armor as well.

- *Dagger +1, +3 versus plants* for 1800gp
- *Long Sword +2* for 8000gp
- *Mace of Disruption* for 30,000gp
- *Halberd +1 to hit, +3 damage* for 5000gp
- *Chain Mail +2* for 8500gp

Ann will offer to coat blades in a special copper alloy she claims is good for strange and unnatural undead. This costs 150gp per weapon and lasts 1d6+4 strikes before wearing off. She has a pot of molten copper ready and is able to do up to 4 weapons before the party is out of time.

Scroll Master - Reedim Ahl

Entering the Scroll Master's establishment, the party members are greeted by a strong musty smell and a sea of scrap parchment everywhere underfoot and running up the 30-foot high shelves.

Reedim is able to make the party up to 3 scrolls for the party for any first or second level spell, though he must climb about his store looking for them.

- First-level spell scroll for 300gp each.
- Second-level spell scroll for 700gp eanch.

He has a discount bin of scrolls where the spells didn't come out right. To anyone looking, they appear right though something feels off.

Examples of how spells could be wrong:

- *Magic Missile* spell that's twice (or half) as potent but only travels half the distance and has no magical guidance, allowing the missiles' target to make a Save vs Wands for no damage.
- *Read Magic* spell that makes the caster say one understanding of what they are reading out loud but have a different understanding in their head, and not knowing which one (or if either) is right.

Reedim is known to have once accidentally created and sold a *Scroll of Jittery Haste*, which each round has a 3-in-6 chance of switching to a *Slow* spell or back to a *Haste* spell.

There is 1-in-20 chance that there's a high-value, powerful spell scroll in the bin that works properly as well as a 1-in-20 chance of a cursed version. For example *Magic Missile* that targets the caster.

Reedim has no interest in helping the party figure out the discount bin scrolls, saying, "Buy them, leave them, I don't care. I have things to write."

General Store - Gotem Ahl

Gotem is the rather bland and unassuming brother of Reedim who runs a sizable general store. Half of his store is currently empty due to supply problems, though he has a decent supply of torches, lanterns, rations, backpacks, and other regular items. That said, they are all for sale at 1d4+1 times the normal price due to scarcity. Behind his counter, he has five vials of special holy water available (able to do 1d4 damage for 1d4 rounds if thrown at an undead) for 100gp each.

Similar to his brother, Gotem has a discount bin. This is filled with used items that have seen better days, such as frayed rope, dented lanterns, etc. The items are offered for standard prices but they have a 2-in-6 chance of failing when needed. If the discount item is food, it has a 2-in-6 chance of being discovered as rotten when eaten (Save vs Poison or take 1d3 damage).

Start

After having two in-game hours in town to get supplies, the party is whisked off in horse-drawn coaches across the peninsula, four horses pulling each one, the bumps of the road making for an uncomfortable and noisy ride. The road to the outskirts of the outpost is at first along well traveled roads and then along a strip of land sandwiched between a mountain range and the ocean.

The grand magistrate, 4 Elite guards, and Yokik accompany the party. It's clear the grand magistrate has put all of his political capital in the party and he believes the fate of Korusk hangs in the balance. Yokik has hinted that she was asked by the chancellor to behead the grand magistrate should the party fail, as well as hunt down the party, something she very much doesn't want to do but is duty-bound to do.

Here are some additional points shared with the party during the trip:

- The three parts of the cannon are hidden in the outpost ruins somewhere. One part is the barrel, another is the special trolley or cart on which it rests, and the last part is the firing mechanism which is the end of the cannon (tail of the cannon with the breech and knob assembly at the end).

- According to military advisors, the best location to shoot the cannon from is the top of the three-story tower. The trajectory should be best for hitting the pirate ship before the pirates make landfall.

- Vocini has a sizable force of loyal pirates and at least two mages on his warship. Their longboats were reported damaged in the naval ambush, so they aren't sure how they would make landfall.

- Yokik shares that there was a great battle a year ago in the sky above the eastern side of the outpost area, and a magical halberd went missing. She's offering a reward of 25,000gp and an item of her own in return for it and allowing it to be put into the Korusk Hall of Champions. It belonged to a now-deceased friend of hers.

As the coach comes to a stop, the grand magistrate tells the party that he will be watching from a safe distance and will pick up the party when they arrive with the cannon. The party has until midnight, more than twelve hours, until the coaches will be forced to return to the capital city. It is a two-to-three-day march back, in good weather.

The grand magistrate presents the party with one small piece of the cannon. "This is a cannon sight McFinly designed for the *Cannons of the Blessed*. It's said to magically enhance the cannon's accuracy. I wish you all the best. Now go. Vocini will arrive in a few hours."

He wishes the party good luck. The coaches pull away, quickly vanishing into the forest.

GM's Notes

Cannon Sight

The magical cannon sight is genuine but has been modified from the original. The sight gives a +2 to hit and allows the lowest damage die to be re-rolled; however, it has another purpose. Once attached, the sight doesn't come off. At midnight, the cannon is deactivated and unable to be used again until a special spell is cast, one known only to the chancellor's chief magical advisor. This is not known to the capital city's grand magistrate or Yokik.

Clock is ticking

In 3-4 hours, Vocini's ship appears on the horizon. It breaks through the distant fog and starts approaching. After another 30-60 minutes, they could make landfall (see the *Structure of the Adventure* section earlier in the adventure).

Dropped off

The party has been dropped off at Area 1 - The North Western Forest. The Area 1 description is located in the *Areas – Outdoors* section below.

Stats for Grand Magistrate

While the stat blocks for Yokik Swiftblade and Elite Guards are in the *Creatures* section, the grand magistrate is a normal person and has an AC 10, 2 HP, and can do 1 point of damage with their fists. He fights as a level 0 fighter (Normal Man).

Fog at sea

The players are able to see a distance out to sea only up to a certain point, which is covered in fog.

Map - Outdoors - West

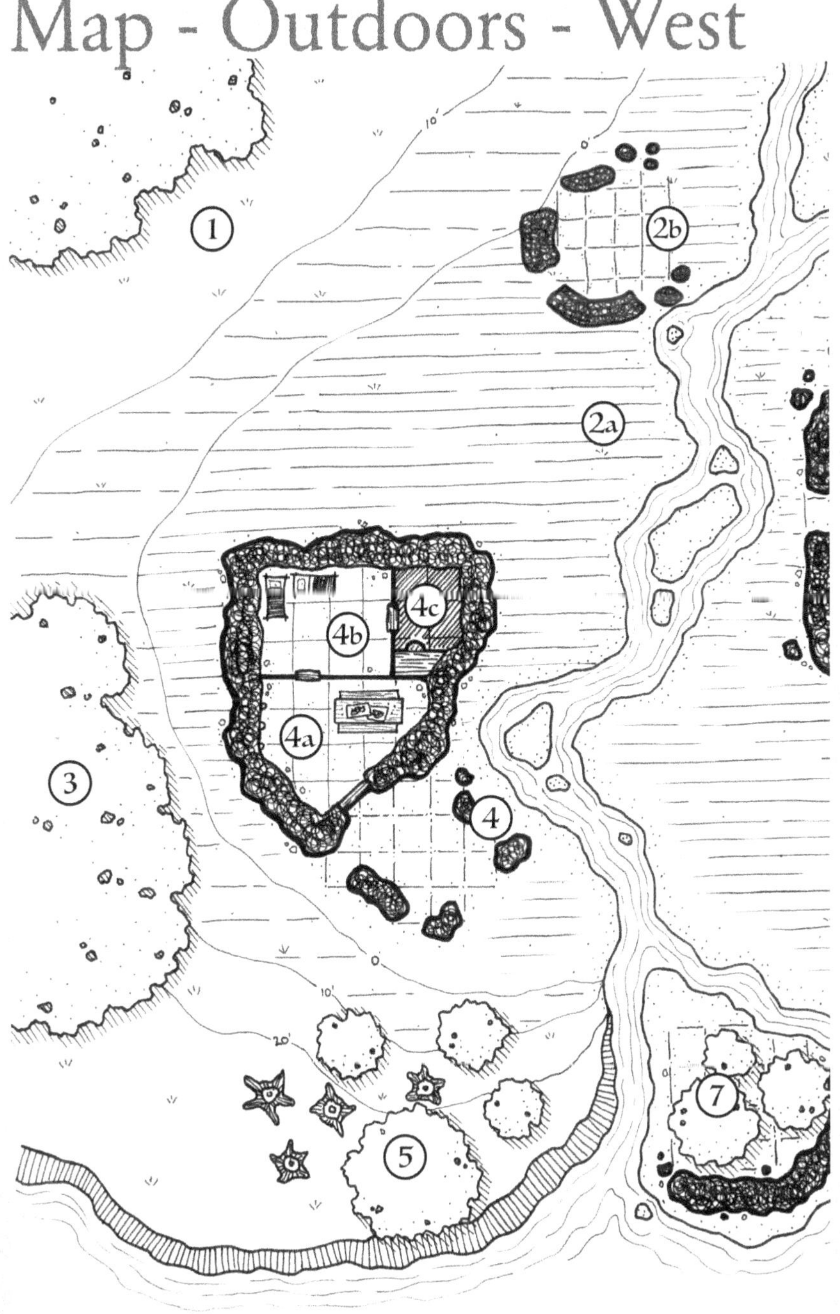

Map - Outdoors - East

Areas - Outdoors

#1 - NORTH-WESTERN FOREST

The forest area to the northwest extends up to the sheer mountain-side, which ascends sharply until it seems to scratch the grey and darkening skies far above. There's a thick cluster of trees to the south that obscures a portion of the party's view of the sea and the deadly drop to the crashing shores below.

The grassy strip of land descends into swampland, forming a putrid basin. It is covered in a sparsely wooded grey-green swamp, with buildings and ruins of the outpost looking like small islands, having been built upon raised stone. There's a thin mist hanging over the basin. The smell of the swamp burns the nose and irritates the eyes.

The outpost appears to consist of:

- Remains of a collapsed tower directly to the east;
- Ruins of another building further to the east, its two-floor-high walls still somewhat intact;
- A single-floor building to the southeast, fully intact;
- A high defensive wall with tall trees near it by the sea edge; and
- A tower on the far side in the southeast that sits above the basin, at or near the same elevation the players are on now.

There appears to be a sparkling, silvery river that cuts through as if the swamp wasn't there.

The only sounds of life are birds chirping to the west and south, and the swamp-filled basin is disturbingly silent.

GM's NOTES

North-Western Forest (Area 1)

There's nothing of particular note in this part of the forest. As a reminder, the party won't see creatures such as Swamp Zomtrees or Swamp Wights walking about in the swamp, unless they are within 90 feet, due to the magical residue in the swamp fog (see *About the Swamp* earlier in the adventure).

Grand Magistrate is Hidden

Even if the party searches, they won't find where the coaches, grand magistrate, and Yokik went, as there is no trail due to magic. A spell has been put on the coaches that cloaks them, which the grand magistrate has control of. It only lasts until the following morning.

If the party is in trouble, the GM may choose to have Yokik Swiftblade attempt to save the day (Yokik's details are in the *Creatures* section at the back of the adventure).

#2A - RIVER

As you trudge across the swamp, a sparkling catches your attention. At first, it seems like it might be an item, but then you notice it cutting across from the mountain to the sea, like a vein of silver or diamond. Finally, you are close enough to see it is a crystal-clear river that emerges from beneath the mountain cliff and slices through the swamp, holding back its foulness until it drops into the sea. Its mist is fresh and welcoming, and pushes aside the putrid and thick air of the swamp.

Though you can see the river raging and spraying, smashing upon rocks, you can barely hear it, as if the river is magically shushed.

Looking about, you can see stepping stones leading to and from the mini-rock islands, providing a safer place to cross.

GM's NOTES

River

If a player gets close enough, they are able to see through to the bottom which is covered in smooth, colorful stones. There are some sparkles of what could be silver and gold peeking out from the pebbled bottom.

The river is goes from two feet deep to three feet in the middle. Its water is drinkable and between the powerful current and the rocks, it is treacherously slippery to traverse.

Crossing the river is best done at the small rock islands (the largest of them is very close to the Area 2a marker on the map). At these small rock islands, there are larger and higher stones that can be used for crossing without the need for a dexterity check if crossed slowly and carefully. Attempting to cross the river anywhere else requires a hard strength check (see *Ability Checks and Difficulty*).

If a character fails a dexterity ability check while crossing:

- They fall prone and take 1d4 damage. Their concentration is disrupted, affecting any prolonged spell or effect.

- They are swept 10' down river and must make a successful strength check (fighting the current) to stop going any further. Success means they are able to crawl out of the river. Failure means they take another 1d4 damage and are swept another 10' down river. They can only move up to 20' per round.

- If they are pushed off the map, they fall 40' and land on sharp rocks with pounding waves (4d10).

Divine Knowledge

Any divine class (Cleric, Paladin, etc.) examining the water may determine it has a holy water quality to it, potentially from a temple or something hidden in the mountain (not part of this adventure).

The river's water is able to do 1d4 damage to Swamp Wights and Swamp Zomtrees, as well as other undead. However, it loses its potency after 1 day.

Swamp Wights and the river

Swamp Wights won't cross the river. After spending a round trying to figure out how to get around it, they will submerge into the swamp water and leave.

Shiny Items

Throughout the river are shiny rocks, pieces of bone, scraps of armor, and broken weapons. Among this detritus are a few items of value:

- A weapons cache with a copper-coated dagger and a magical throwing dagger (+2 to hit);

- The trick hilt of a sword that's actually a blade-trap, which causes 2d4 damage when picked up and resets with each attempt to grab it;

- The *Ring of Thudisi* (see *Magical Items*) on a skeletal hand; and

- A scroll case with a ruined scroll inside.

Attempting to pick up any item requires both a dexterity check and a strength check to fight the current and stay balanced — unless the players come up with a better plan.

2B - CRUMBLED TOWER

In its prime, the top of the crumbled tower likely rose above the tree-line giving an amazing view, but those days are long gone. What remains is a ground floor and parts of the tower wall with supports for a second floor and a single, rotting beam hinting at a floor above that. It's impossible to tell whether it was age, cannon fire, or another fate that humbled the tower, but it is clear that it has been in a sorry state for quite some time.

There are a few twisted, wilted trees and a few dead ones about, likely part of a garden at some point, now covered by swamp.

An odd crunching sound is coming from the other side of a piece of the tower's wall.

GM's NOTES

Enemies lurking

On the other side of the wall are two Swamp Wights eating the remains of someone who had fallen off the cliff earlier that day. There's a camouflaged Swamp Zomtree looking like a dead tree, watching and waiting for prey of its own.

Swamp Wights

AC 5 [14], HD 3 (13 HP), Att 1x claws (1d8) or infectious touch, THAC0 17 [+2], MV 120' (40'), SV D12 W13 P14 B15 S16 (3), ML 12, AL Chaotic Evil, XP 50, NA 2d4 (1d8+2),TT B, Abilities: Undead and Plant Vulnerability, Physical Immunity , Silent Killer, Sense Living (90'), Infectious Touch (drain 1d6 CON), Unimpeded

Swamp Zomtree

AC 2 [17], HD 7 (32 HP), Att 2x branch claws (2d6 each), THAC0 12 [+7], MV 60' (20'), SV D8 W9 P10 B10 S12 (8), ML 9, AL Chaotic Evil, XP 650, NA 1d4 (1d8), TT C, Abilities: Unholy Scream, Undead and Plant Vulnerabilities, Immunity, Camouflage, Extended Reach

---

At first sight of the party, the wights attack. The Swamp Swamp Zomtree, however, waits for the right moment to ambush the party.

Treasure

A persistent search of the remains of the tower reveals a partially submerged, small, lacquered wooden chest. It needs to be pried open with a strength of 13+ or be smashed open, which could result in damaging the items or losing them in the swamp. Inside the chest:

- *1 Ring of the Arborist* (see *Magical Items*)
- *1 Vial of Potent Healing* (see *Magical Items*)
- 2 rubies, each the size of a child's fist and worth 500gp each

3 - PILE IN THE FOREST

Peering into the very thick section of forest, you can see a poorly-made ladder nailed to a tree and a sad, warped, rotten wood platform high up in the branches. It was likely used as a lookout above the canopy of the forest long ago; however, the forest has grown since then.

A glint of metal draws attention to a large, unnatural mound of dead branches and dried-out bushes in the middle of the forest.

GM's NOTES

Pile

When a player is within 10' of the mound (located where the Area 3 label is on the map), they can see a skeletal leg and arm sticking out of the pile. Inside it are a dozen dead soldiers. The corpses are in weather-beaten, old uniforms of the nation of Korusk. It is clear that they had suffered a grisly fate, as the bones and bodies appear smashed or blown to bits.

There is a pile of rusted and damaged weapons hidden in the mound as well.

Touching the pile

If anyone touches the mound, a *Magic Mouth* appears and says the following:

"The price has doubled, you backstabbing skunk. Again, we negotiated in good faith, and again, you attempt to steal what we had rightfully stolen and rightfully offer.

"I'm leaving this here for whatever fools you send next, so that they know what fate awaits them. Pay, or I swear on my baby son Vocini's life, we shall scatter the parts of the cannon and you will lose your chancellorship. I have left the cannon's sight in the small black-and-silver chest as proof that really have one of McFinly's weapons.

"And do not think that we will surrender out of fear of the Sea Witch. Her wrath is merely bothersome."

No Chest and the weapons pile

There is no small black-and-silver chest around, and there is nothing of value on the bodies. Their uniforms are threadbare and stained. Here are the contents of the pile:

- 4 dull halberds (-1 to hit, -1 damage)
- 10 dull long swords (-2 damage)
- 5 broken short bows (unusable)
- 4 badly bashed shields (no protection)
- 40 semi-usable arrows (-1 to hit because of warping)
- 1 *Scythe +2 vs Plants (treat as two-handed weapon, 1d8 damage)*
- 4 *Arrows +1*

4 - Outside of the Main Building

This structure is built on a natural stone foundation, which rises six inches above the swamp and looks like a flat stone island. Its walls are made from cliff rock and mortar that has been repaired time and again. The thatch roof has plants growing out of it.

Over the entrance is a wooden sign with the engraved and painted word "Main" on it, though it hard to see, having been badly weathered. Its door is thick, aged wood with lots of scars and burn marks.

Floating back and forth in front of the main building is a ghostly figure, muttering to itself. It appears to be an upset, gaunt, scraggly bearded man in tattered clothing. It's in a state of decay and has ghostly plants growing out of his limbs and out one eye socket.

GM's Notes

Ghost

The specter is muttering several things that can be overheard and understood by the party if they listen carefully:

- "Why hasn't Reginald come back yet? He said he was coming back in two days. It's been two weeks. We should leave."

- "Should we move the barrel? Reginald said put it in the barracks, we put it there, but now it burnt down. He's going to be mad. He's going to blame me for burning it down. Oh, he'll be mad."

- "The swamp water rose again, I saw it. We have to let the Sea Witch go. It's not right to have her down there, stuffed underground. She doesn't even know her friend died."

- "I think she's making the monsters, like the one that killed Daytoe last night."

- "The bodies, so many bodies piling up. Why do bad people keep coming to steal our cannon? I'm hungry."

The ghost is a swamp specter and ignores the party unless he is either attacked or spoken to.

Talking with the ghost

If spoken to nicely or treated with kindness, it breaks out of its confused state and thanks the person. It will then offer important information to the players before again being lost to its confused thoughts.

- His name is Ubik. He knows something is wrong, doesn't know he's dead, and feels hungry, tired, and scared. He believes he is on watch, protecting the building, waiting for Reginald to return. He believes it's an important building.

- He was of a low rank, one of the original outpost soldiers. His boss made a deal with the traitorous crew. He believes it's okay because they don't get paid much. He doesn't think they are asking for much, but he doesn't know.

- His leader was Captain Reginald. An official carriage came to take him and the pirate captain to negotiate. They took half the crew with them. It's been weeks, yet neither of them have returned.

- Ubik is angry about the Sea Witch. "They have to let the Sea Witch go. It's not right. McFinly's dead anyway, and she doesn't even know." He rubs his head incessantly when talking about this and then stops, saying, "I have to do it. I have to tell her." He then walks several paces before forgetting what he's doing.

- If the party has been looking for a part of the cannon with no success, he'll point them in the right direction.

If the party is kind to him a second time (at least 30 minutes elapsed between each visit), even if it's just a kind word like "Hello, Ubik", he shows genuine appreciation and grants the player who said it a blessing of +1 to saving throws for the remainder of this adventure. This only works once.

Attacking the ghost

If Ubik is threatened or struck at with a magical weapon, he'll scream and 1d4+1 Swamp Wights rise out of the swamp and attack the party to defend him. After 3 rounds, Ubik disappears. He returns an hour later as if nothing had happened, for he has no memory of anything.

Swamp Specter (Ubik)

*AC 0 [19], HD 10** (45 HP), Att 1 touch (life drain) or 2x spectral claws (2d6 damage each), THAC0 11 [+8], MV 90' (30'), SV D6 W7 P8 B8 S10 (10), ML 10, AL Any, XP 2750, TT E, N Abilities: Undead and Plant Vulnerability, Physical Immunity, Silent Killer, Fright, Life drain, Spectral Claws*

Swamp Wights

AC 5 [14], HD 3 (13 HP), Att 1x claws (1d8) or infectious touch, THAC0 17 [+2], MV 120' (40'), SV D12 W13 P14 B15 S16 (3), ML 12, AL Chaotic Evil, XP 50, NA 2d4 (1d8+2),TT B, Abilities: Undead and Plant Vulnerability, Physical Immunity, Sense Living (90'), Infectious Touch (drain 1d6 CON), Unimpeded

---

Fate of the Sea Witch

If the Sea Witch is freed, then Ubik is gone, leaving behind only a palpable sense of relief.

If the Sea Witch is killed, Ubik goes mad and attacks the party at first sight.

4A - FRONT OFFICE

The door is made of thick wood with metal reinforcements at the edges and around the middle. The door is covered in numerous scars. There are broken arrow heads, cleaving marks, and a large set of circular indents potentially from a small battering ram. If the door could talk, it would likely tell a tale or two.

As it opens, it creaks loudly and wobbles. You are greeted with the strong smell of mildew and ash.

Dominating the room is a large table with two bench seats. Decorating the table are discolored flagons, empty tin plates, open books, and curled papers. On the northern wall are maps and other papers, held in place with rusted nails.

The ceiling has planks of wood under the thatch. There are several arrows stuck in it.

Interestingly, there are no windows. Apart from the entrance door, there's only a door to the north.

You notice some strange, small, bright purple flowers growing on thin, sickly green vines that hide in the shadows where the walls meet the floor and ceiling. You spot one under the floor boards through a knot. Perhaps the building isn't on so much of an island, and the swamp had found its way in.

GM's Notes

The table

Under the table is a bucket of rusted nails and a small rusted hammer (no value).

On the table are papers from five sets of documents.

- **Duty roster.** There's a list of who is on duty, who is on leave, who is coming.

- **Overture.** There's a letter in exquisite penmanship on heavy paper with a gold seal signed as McFinly. It proposes to allow her envoy to land and discuss working together. Apparently there was a gift of some kind that was provided to incentivize them and releasing the prisoner was required as a show of good faith.

- **Supplies List.** There are two sets of papers that are similar. One shows what you gather is an inventory of official supplies and the other a second, different copy of the inventory that also included barrels of wine and weapons. There are also two sets of accounting ledgers.

- **Tactical note.** There's a note with a hole in it, likely having been pinned to the wall at one point. The handwriting looks angry. The note says: "Where's the tactician notebook, Gerald? You have to put things back!"

- **Desperate correspondence.** There's a letter in an envelope hidden between two floor boards, as if it had fallen. It's in terrible, shaky handwriting. It talks about losing men daily and despite having

blown up the building above the Sea Witch, still her magic plagues them. It mentions that they haven't been able to find Ubik and that they figure he's among some deserters.

Hidden among the papers is a *Scroll of Invisibility to Plants*. This makes one target invisible to any of the swamp creatures for 10 minutes. However, if any hostile action is taken toward a swamp creature, the spell ends.

Map Wall

There are several generations of maps on the wall, but only a few interesting ones.

- **Original area map**. This map shows the plans for the outpost which includes a barracks and jailhouse, a building to the east of the current one.
- **Updated plans**. These plans show a large area to dig out, under the jailhouse.
- **Gibby's number**. There's a simple looking map of the outpost with an arrow pointing to a cluster of trees at the edge and some words scrawled: "Stump. Gibby's number. Fake bottom."

Vines and flowers

The vines are not part of a Swamp Zomtree; however, if the vines are attacked, or the flowers are plucked, the plant will squirt a liquid at those within 5 feet of it. Those affected must roll a Save vs Paralysis or be paralyzed for 10 minutes.

If a flower is successfully removed from the plant, it can be used to coat a weapon with the paralytic poison, however it won't affect the swamp creatures. The poison is good for 2 hits and only lasts 1 hour. Plucked flowers last a day.

Doors

The door to 4b is heavily reinforced wood and metal, similar to the one entering this room. There is a trap in Area 4c that causes both of the doors to close and lock.

Someone who successfully attempts to *Find Traps* discovers there's a mechanism that affects both doors, but it's not clear what it does or how it is triggered.

When the doors are closed and the lock has been picked, opening the doors requires a total strength of 20 or more to and takes two rounds as the mechanism is trying to force the doors closed. Ten minutes after being triggered, the mechanism

stops. Alternatively, the hinges on the doors can take 30 HP of damage before coming off.

4B - OLD ARMORY AND BARRACKS

The door opens with some hesitation, as if the wood has swollen from moisture or if some mechanism were working hard to push it closed.

In the room are two beds and hooks with items along one wall: shields, helmets, swords, bows. The hooks appear to be grouped into five sections, each one with a name plate above it. There are metal braces on the door and adjacent walls to support putting in a beam for extra protection, though there is no beam about.

The beds are wooden and are clearly poorly made, with the pieces of wood not having been finished and not lining up properly. Even from a distance you can tell there are too many nails used. There's a strange, shiny sheen on them, as if the pillow and blankets had been coated in putrid sugar.

There's a thick-looking door of dark wood to the east. Part of the floor at the edge of the door is blackened. The air has a damp, moldy spell with a stronger smell of ash mixed in.

GM's Notes

Name plates

There are engraved tin name plates above the five hooks: Farvosh 819, Biggy 117, Gibby 447, Gerald 420, Arto 513, Daytoe 390.

The name plates are affixed with loose nails. There are another dozen or so name plates in a pile on the floor.

Underneath the beds

Under one bed is a copper-coating kit consisting of a small bucket with hardened copper in it and a sharp-edged spade used to scrape off the excess. If the party can magically heat up the copper to where it liquifies there's enough to coat up to three weapons for 10 hits each. There's a note explaining how to do it and saying that coated weapons "seems to hurt those bastards."

There is a notebook under the other bed with pages with battle plans regarding how ships tend to attack the outpost. There are a number of calculations and diagrams, all leading to the conclusion that the best place from which to fire the cannon is the second floor, not the third floor, of the tower.

Weapons and armor

There are 3 rusty short swords, two rusty long swords, a warped bow, a *Bow +1*, two helms, and three small shields. Other than the magical bow, these items are battered and bent, and are useless in combat.

Hidden ring

A careful search reveals a ring lodged between the stones of the floor. It's a *Ring of Encounters* (see *Magical Items*), made of black and twisted vines.

Door to Area 4c

This door is similar to the one entering this room, also heavily reinforced wood and metal. It, too, has a mechanism that can be triggered from 4c to cause it to slam close and lock, which can be discovered with a successful *Find Traps* check.

When closed and the lock has been picked, the door requires a total strength of 20 or more to open it and will take 2 rounds to do so. Alternatively, its hinges can be destroyed with 30 HP of damage, or the party can wait 10 minutes for the mechanism to unlock and release the doors.

4c - Office

The heavy door resists being opened even more than the previous door. As it opens, there's a violent stench of ash and decay that assaults your senses.

The walls, ceiling, and floor here are scorched black. The top layer of wood has bubbled up looking like they are made of thin sheets of black paper. Scattered about on the floor are curled remnants of paper and a small skeleton.

Looking to the south, there appears to be a short makeshift desk made of a small sheet of metal laying on top of something oddly shaped. There are stone tiles leaning against the desk as well.

There is a four-foot-high metal lever coming out of the floor in the north-eastern corner of the room. It's more than two inches thick and once may have had intricate etchings, but those seem to have been worn, or melted, away.

GM's Notes

Lever

The metal lever is broken and comes out of the floor easily. It can be used as a poor-quality quarterstaff (-1 to hit).

It used to control the mechanism for the doors, but has been replaced by the desk trap.

Trapped desk

The sheet of metal is hiding a black chest and is resting on top of the trolley part of the *Cannon of the Blessed*. The trolley is on its side, its wheels facing the far wall.

The stone tiles obscure seeing under much of the desk and are trapped. If the third of the four tiles is moved, the desk trap is set off.

- **Doors.** The doors to 4a and 4b close and lock. See their descriptions about attempting to open the doors.

- **Timer.** A strange ticking starts. After three rounds, a fireball detonates in 4c. All players and NPCs in the room suffer 4d6 but may Save vs Breath Weapon for half damage.

- **Reset.** After 10 minutes, the doors will unlock and be able to be opened normally, and the trap resets.

A successful *Disarm Trap* addresses both the closing/locking mechanism as well as the fireball.

Black chest

The black stone chest supporting the desk is two feet wide by two feet tall, perfectly covered in ash. It contains:

- 2 small gems (100gp each),

- 2 *Potions of Cure Serious Wounds* (2d6+1)

- 1 wineskin with wonderful smelling wine, which is poisoned. Drinking it requires a Save vs Poison or be blinded for 1d4 hours (-4 to hit, -4 to AC).

5 - STUMPS AND TREES

This area looks out at the sea. Four large trees stretch up at least fifty feet into the air and are accompanied by four wide tree stumps that appear to have chunks out of them, likely from axe throwing or some other pastime. There are several fallen trees covered in moss.

Beyond the largest of the trees, the land plunges dramatically down to the sea. It is a drop of at least twenty feet. The waves crash and play against the well-polished rocks below.

The ground here is firm and grassy rather than swampy, though two of the smaller trees look sickly. Perhaps the swamp has receded or perhaps it has penetrated the ground water.

A wooden lookout platform sits between three of the trees, about twenty feet up. There's a battered, poor-quality wooden ladder laying on the ground, partially coated in swamp slime.

GM's Notes

Suspicious fallen trees

Among the fallen trees are two Swamp Zomtrees waiting to attack the party.

> **Swamp Zomtree**
> *AC 2 [17], HD 7 (32 HP), Att 2x branch claws (2d6 each), THAC0 12 [+7], MV 60' (20'), SV D8 W9 P10 B10 S12 (8), ML 9, AL Chaotic Evil, XP 650, NA 1d4 (1d8), TT C, Abilities: Unholy Scream, Undead and Plant Vulnerabilities, Immunity, Camouflage, Extended Reach*

Ladder and platform

The ladder has a 4-in-6 chance of collapsing if used and won't support more than 250 pounds.

The platform itself is brittle. It is made of rotten wood planks and is likely to give way at any moment (3-in-6 chance of collapsing per round). From here, a character could see that there's a glint of something on the top of the wall in Area 7.

The platform cannot support the cannon.

Stumps

Upon close inspection of the stumps, a perceptive player (optional wisdom check) notices one of them is different from the others. It appears a bit more square-shaped, looking more crafted than a real stump.

Further examination reveals that the top part of the odd stump can be opened, and coded dials and a small metal handle are found inside. It is currently set to 818.

The correct code is Gabby's number from Area 4b: 447. If that code is entered and the handle is pulled, it opens a storage area.

If a different code is set and the handle pulled, it will deliver a shock for 1d8.

Attempting to break open the stump is an option, but it requires 60 HP of damage to get through.

The contents of the stump are:

- 1 sack with 400gp, another with 100sp
- 1 sack with two gems (100gp, 300gp)
- 2 fine-looking daggers with copper edges (50gp each)
- 3 *Potions of Cure Light Wounds* (1d6+1)
- *Wand of Magic Missiles* with 15 charges

At the bottom of the storage area is a piece of black cloth under which can be seen scratch marks at the edges. The false bottom can be pried out with a dagger and reveals the firing mechanism for the *Cannon of the Blessed*. The mechanism weighs 100 pounds.

Firing the Cannon

If the party decides to try and fire the cannon from this area, they have a -3 penalty to hit, as they don't have enough height.

Pirate Landfall

When it's time for Vocini's crew to make landfall (see *Structure of the Adventure - Part 4 Pirate Landfall* earlier in the adventure), two pirates armed with spyglasses will be monitoring the coastline. Any party members out in the open have a 2-in-6

chance of being noticed and drawing cannon fire 1d3 rounds later.

The target of the barrage must make a Save vs Breath Weapon or suffer 4d6 damage (save for half). Anyone within 30 feet of the target takes 2d6 damage on a failed saving throw or none with a successful one. A barrage results in 1d3 rounds of a dust and dirt cloud, obscuring another shot and giving players time to get away.

For details about the portals and pirates, see *Vocini and Crew* in the *Creatures* section.

The Drop

The drop off the edge is actually forty feet and anyone venturing off will take 4d10 damage landing on sharp rocks and being smashed with crashing waves.

6A - COLLAPSED TWO-STORY BUILDING

As you approach the remains of the once proud, two-story building, you notice it is set on a raised stone foundation, keeping it just beyond the reach of the swamp. There are symbols and logos on the outside of the walls. There appears to be the remains of a separate, smaller building to the north.

The walls of the building are three feet thick and go up at least twenty feet. Inside there are a few sagging, warped, and charred beams that formed the second floor and other beams that would have supported a peaked roof. The beams are supported by what looks like an array of metal black posts positioned in a grid pattern, spaced every ten feet. The two-foot thick posts appear to be more recent than the rest of the structure, potentially an attempt to preserve the second floor at some point or to rebuild.

There are dark vines running along the walls, pushed up floor tiles, and wrapped around some of the beams, as if the swamp wanted its presence to be felt.

GM's NOTES
Symbols and logos

Any warrior type, like fighters, can tell from symbols on the outside of the building that it was a barracks. The insignias present different companies over time, and the symbols

indicate how many of what type of troops were housed there. The last number is a one, for only one soldier had remained.

Interior

The black pillars are made of a thick metal. They are hollow and likely were built to support a very heavy second floor, though there's no longer any part of the second floor left. Where the ninth pillar would be is a sickly looking tree, its roots having burrowed into the tiles. The tree is the same height as the black pillars but is twice as thick. Its leaves are limp and brown.

Everything appears covered in black soot. There is a strange burnt smell permeating the area.

There's a pile of left over black pillars, tiles, and other debris in the northeastern corner. A skeleton, its armor melted to slag, rests among the rubble.

Southern wall - outside

On the outer part of the south wall are the faded remnants of painted official Korusk crests and emblems, an indication of what faction or group controlled this outpost at one time or another.

Enemies waiting

The south-eastern-most post is actually part of a giant Swamp Zomtree disguised as a smaller, sickly trunk. Its roots are spread throughout the building's floors and walls. These roots are drawn in if and when the giant Swamp Zomtree decides to attack the party. Two of the metal posts have regular Swamp Zomtrees hidden inside them.

The giant Swamp Zomtree is the leader and attacks when it feels it is threatened or when it feels it can gain surprise. At that time, it grows to its full height of 20 feet, knocking the remaining planks for the second floor flying. It attacks those who look like spellcasters or priests first. The other two Swamp Zomtrees join in and attack anyone.

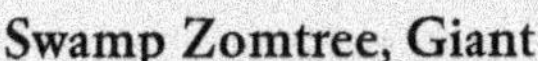

Swamp Zomtree, Giant

AC 1 [18], HD 8 (40 HP), Att 4x branch claws (2d6 each), THAC0 12 [+7], MV 60' (20'), SV D8 W9 P10 B10 S12 (8), ML 9, AL Chaotic Evil, XP 750, NA 1d2 (1d4), TT None, Abilities: Entangle, Undead and Plant Vulnerability, Immunity, Camouflage, Swamp Portal, Extended Reach

Swamp Zomtree

AC 2 [17], HD 7 (32 HP), Att 2x branch claws (2d6 each), THAC0 12 [+7], MV 60' (20'), SV D8 W9 P10 B10 S12 (8), ML 9, AL Chaotic Evil, XP 650, NA 1d4 (1d8), TT C, Abilities: Unholy Scream, Undead and Plant Vulnerabilities, Immunity, Camouflage, Extended Reach

The pile and the Cannon barrel

Upon investigation by the party, they discover that in the pile of building supplies is a strange looking, long, thick post. It is the barrel of the *Cannon of the Blessed*, which had been painted to disguise it.

There are some symbols on the wall which a magical spellcaster (like an illusionist, magic-user, or race-as-class elf) can recognize as being a magical language. If they use *Read Magic*, they learn it says: "Don't be like Gilberto. Disarm first."

The barrel has a wire trigger which detonates a fireball. If the trap is triggered, or a disarm trap attempt fails, all those within 20 feet will take 4d6 damage or Save vs Breath Weapon for half.

Carrying the barrel

The barrel is remarkably heavy, weighing 300 pounds, and is remarkably awkward to carry. If two players are carrying it together, they have a -2 penalty to dexterity check and AC, and move at ½ speed.

Someone attempting to drag the barrel by themselves must have a strength of 15 or higher and has a penalty of -3 to dexterity check and AC, and moves at ¼ speed.

If the cannon is dropped into the swamp, it takes 1d10 minutes to find it. The swamp doesn't want the *Cannon of the Blessed* to

be removed so it slowly moves the cannon away from the party.

6B - CRUMBLED EXTENSION

There are scant remains of the smaller, secondary building. Pieces of the walls, which were barely a foot thick, are scattered about in a radial pattern. There's no wood or hint of the roof, only the stone tile platform that it was built on, along with the larger building to the immediate south.

The only thing of note is a circle of rocks around stone tiles with ashen wood and debris in the middle, looking like a large campfire.

GM's NOTES

Secret Passage

Under the tiles of the campfire is an entrance to the smuggler's lair and underground prison. This is treated as a secret passage for purposes of detection.

Removing the tiles reveals a ladder that goes down into complete darkness and Area 11 (see the *Underground Map*). The passage is dark and smells foul, with fumes that make the eyes water.

When that tile is lifted up, 5 Swamp Wights rise up from the surrounding swamp and attack them. They are dressed in decayed pirate garb.

> **Swamp Wights**
>
> *AC 5 [14], HD 3 (13 HP), Att 1x claws (1d8) or infectious touch, THAC0 17 [+2], MV 120' (40'), SV D12 W13 P14 B15 S16 (3), ML 12, AL Chaotic Evil, XP 50, NA 2d4 (1d8+2),TT B, Abilities: Undead and Plant Vulnerability, Physical Immunity , Silent Killer, Sense Living (90'), Infectious Touch (drain 1d6 CON), Unimpeded*

7 - TREES AND THE WALL

Cut off by the crystal-clear river, this little island on the edge has stone tiles partially upended with tree roots and a large, defensive wall.

The defensive rock-and-mortar wall is over five feet thick and covered in a black mildewy film. There are arrow slits every few feet and handholds that go up to the top of the wall.

The ground has tufts of grass in a few places but looks like most of it was trampled.

GM's Notes

Strange footprints

A tracker or ranger-type character can notice that the ground's been trampled by a single set of footprints, likely human. It's as if they have walked over the area for years. The tracks lead to the sea-facing side of the defensive wall.

Trapped Soldier

On the seaside of the defensive wall is a gaunt, withered figure clutching to the wall with clawed hands. He is staring out at the sea, being seared by the sun's rays which are causing him agony. If he notices anyone, he will hiss and ask sharply who's there. He threatens to throw himself into the sea.

The soldier was half-transformed into a Swamp Wight before having retreated to the small island, where he was cut off from the Sea Witch's power. He was the last soldier and has been trying to die for decades, unable to leave the tiny island and unable to let go of the wall.

If spoken to, he asks to be killed and shares what little he remembers.

- **Reginald's fate.** He saw Captain Reginald's body on the rocks below, so he figured the pirate captain did it.

- **Why this island?** One of his friends turned into a swamp creature and attacked him, which is how he ended up on the rock island.

- **Carriage ambush.** He was part of the group that ambushed the carriage and hid it on the eastern side, against the mountain. He doesn't know why they had to kill those people but figures they left them there because there were lots of spies.

- **Sea wall.** He loved walking on top of the wall, looking out to the edge of the world.

If the party attacks him, he apologies and attacks them back - he can't control himself.

If the party tries to abandon him, he gets angry and attacks.

If the party offers to help get him off the small rock island and return him back to the swamp, he is grateful. He then tells the party about a nook in a tree where they will find a magical potion taken from the carriage. It's a *Toxin of the Ghoul* (see *Magical Items*).

Modified Swamp Wight - Last soldier
AC 6 [13], HD 3 (15 HP), Att 1x claws (1d8) or infectious touch, THAC0 17 [+2], MV 120' (40'), SV D12 W13 P14 B15 S16 (3), ML 12, AL Chaotic Evil, XP 50, NA 2d4 (1d8+2),TT B, Abilities: Undead and Plant Vulnerability, Physical Immunity

---

Loose stone

If someone climbs up the wall, they find a loose top stone, under which is a *Spyglass of the Pathfinder* (see *Magical Items*) and a note that reads: Put it back when yer done. Don't be a Gerald.

Firing the cannon

If the party decides to try and fire the cannon from here, they have a -3 to hit as they don't have enough height. In addition, they have to put the cannon dangerously close to the cliff to try and fire around the wall. If fired, the cannon has a 3-in-6 chance of falling off the edge and into the sea below.

Pirate landfall

When it's time for Vocini's crew to make landfall (see *Structure of the Adventure - Part 4 Pirate Landfall*), the mages aboard the ship open two portals as two pirates aboard monitor the coast with spyglasses for potential threats.

Unless party members are on the top of the defensive wall or on the wall's water-facing side, they won't be spotted by the ship and shot at. If they are seen, then 1d3 rounds after being spotted, the ship fires its cannons. The target of the barrage must make a Save vs Breath Weapon or suffer 4d6 damage (save for half). Anyone within 30 feet of the target takes 2d6 damage or none with a successful save. A barrage results in 1d3 rounds of heavy dust or swamp fog, obscuring another shot and giving time to get away.

If the coast is clear and it's time, then one of the portals opens here, and pirates start streaming out. For details about the portals and pirates, see *Vocini and Crew* in the *Creatures* section.

8 - Swamp, swamp, everywhere

The subtle fog that permeates the entire area is thicker here, rising like haunting steam from the green-grey ooze. You stop advancing as your foot plunges significantly deeper into the swamp than before.

You hear unnerving guttural moans in the distance but can't see anything. Ahead of you, is a large pile of tree trunks and branches forming some kind of nest. There are sickly trees here and there throughout the swamp.

Beyond the nest, is the sheer mountain cliff to the north, the sea to the south, and the seemingly endless swamp eastward. The swamp water seems calm, almost still.

GM's Notes

Swamp Depth

Within 20 feet of the nest, the swamp becomes 4 feet deep. This reduces movement for medium-sized characters by 75% and gives an AC penalty of -2. Small-sized characters may become submerged completely under the swamp water and can drown.

Nest and the bait

As the party gets close to the nest, a glint of shiny metal catches their attention. Warrior types can make an intelligence check to recognize it as part of a halberd.

The nest's sides rise two feet above the swamp water level. There's a heap of things covered in swamp slime in the nest, the halberd lodged in the middle shining brightly.

This is a trap. Surrounding the nest are two large crocodiles and four regular ones, along with two giant Swamp Zomtrees. Once someone goes into the nest to investigate, they attack *unless* the party has saved the Sea Witch. If she was saved, they do nothing.

Crocodile, Regular

AC:5 [14], HD 2 (9 HP), Att 1x bite (1d8), THAC0 18 [+1], MV 90' (30'), SV D12 W13 P14 B15 S16 (1), ML 7, AL Neutral, XP: 20

Crocodile, Large

These crocodiles are 25 feet long.

AC:3 [16], HD 6 (30 HP), Att 1x bite (1d8), THAC0 14 [+5], MV 90' (30'), SV D12 W13 P14 B15 S16 (3), ML 7, AL Neutral, XP: 275

Swamp Zomtree, Giant

AC 1 [18], HD 8 (40 HP), Att 4x branch claws (2d6 each), THAC0 12 [+7], MV 60' (20'), SV D8 W9 P10 B10 S12 (8), ML 9, AL Chaotic Evil, XP 750, NA 1d2 (1d4), TT None, Abilities: Entangle, Undead and Plant Vulnerability, Immunity, Camouflage, Swamp Portal, Extended Reach

Heap and treasure

The heap is a pile of dead bodies ranging from the founding of the outpost to one only a week old. Standing out and grabbing attention is a magical halberd that is very firmly stuck into the floor of the swamp. The halberd is the *Halberd of the Storm* (*see Magical Items*) and is the item that Yokik is offering a special reward for. It requires a successful strength check to dislodge.

The nest contains:

- 6 *Arrows +2*
- *Large Shield +1*
- 3 *Potions of Cure Serious Wounds* (2d6+1)
- 2 *Scrolls of Magic Missile*
- A letter with badly smudged writing.

Any character with an intelligence of 13 and above can read the letter. It mentions blowing up the jail and hoping that would bury the Sea Witch.

9 - Wreckage

At first, it looks like there are simply boulders of various sizes that have fallen from on high that have piled up. Upon further investigation, you notice a carriage wheel peeking out from behind a boulder.

Peering through the swamp fog, you see a half-submerged, badly damaged carriage, similar in size and shape to the ones you took to get here. There are arrows and scorch marks all over it.

The threadbare and stained curtains prevent you from seeing inside.

GM's Notes

Carriage

Anyone with a wisdom of 14 or higher can tell that the carriage is rather old from the type of decorations and style, dating it back at least fifty years. The style, however, is an ancestor of the one used on the carriage the party was transported in.

An intelligence check reveals the carriage appears to have been intentionally pushed behind the large boulders to keep it hidden at ground level. A savvy player can discover it would be easily visible from on a mountain ledge high above, perhaps with a spyglass. Looking on the roof shows stains in the shape of a skull.

Inside the carriage is a skeleton in old regal clothing of Korusk, clearly an emissary of some kind. They have two crossbow bolts through their chest pinning them to their seat. A dagger is lodged in the skeleton's skull pinning a piece of paper with a broken wax seal on it.

Caught in the skeleton's trousers, just above the swamp water level, is a sapphire ring worth 500gp.

Pinned paper

The piece of paper is a letter from the first chancellor. It states that the previous offers had been revoked and that the group was to surrender the cannon and themselves immediately to the emissary and the dozen elite guards.

There are no other bodies about.

Hidden staff

Slotted behind the seat, and wrapped in a dark leather cloth matching the seat, is a sapphire-topped *Staff of Submission* (see *Magical Items*).

Hidden letter

Trapped in the under-carriage is a steel box, whose lock needs to be picked. Inside is a letter to the emissary from the chancellor, which states for the emissary is to offer the modified cannon sight to the ruffians as a sign of good faith and how, in the morning, it should be safe to approach them with the forces hidden in the western forest.

10 - TOWER

Even in its dilapidated condition, the tower still commands respect. It stands at over sixty feet tall and is thirty feet wide. Despite being badly battered, with large chunks of its curved, dark brick, outer wall missing, there's a sense of grandness to it. It feels significantly older than the rest of the outpost.

From the ground, you can see parts of the second and top floor missing. On the second floor, you can see what appears to be drapes flapping in what was once a window but is now a gaping wound in the structure.

The first several feet of its structure are covered in swamp ooze, and the steps to its doorless, smashed-open entrance is slick and covered in swamp slime.

GM's Notes

Mage's tower

When magical spellcaster types get to the steps of the tower, they sense it was once a power mage's tower. The spellcasters feel the need to be cautious as who knows what dangers lurk inside.

Climbing the exterior

The exterior of the tower is very slick and precarious to climb. Between decaying bricks ready to give way and a coating of slime, anyone attempting to climb the wall would find it hard (see *Ability Checks and Difficulty*). For every 20 feet, a new climbing attempt roll should be made. Failure requires a strength check or the player falls and takes 1d6 damage per 10 feet.

Blocked exit

Once the party has entered, 2d4 Swamp Wights appear outside. There is a giant Swamp Zomtree wrapped around the tower who joins them. What they do depends on the situation.

- If the party has rescued the Sea Witch, they protect the party from the pirates when/if they make landfall. Any divine (Cleric, Paladin, etc) get an immediate sense that the creatures are there to help.

- If the party killed the Sea Witch, or left her to rot, the wights enter when the party has reached the second floor, with another 1d4 Swamp Wights appearing and waiting outside to ambush the party should they leave. The giant Swamp Zomtree attacks anyone who draws back the drapes of the second floor or appears on the top floor.

- If they haven't encountered the Sea Witch yet, then the creatures lurk while the party is in the tower - visible but not yet taking action.

Swamp Zomtree, Giant

AC 1 [18], HD 8 (40 HP), Att 4x branch claws (2d6 each), THAC0 12 [+7], MV 60' (20'), SV D8 W9 P10 B10 S12 (8), ML 9, AL Chaotic Evil, XP 750, NA 1d2 (1d4), TT None, Abilities: Entangle, Undead and Plant Vulnerability, Immunity, Camouflage, Swamp Portal, Extended Reach

Swamp Wights

AC 5 [14], HD 3 (13 HP), Att 1x claws (1d8) or infectious touch, THAC0 17 [+2], MV 120' (40'), SV D12 W13 P14 B15 S16 (3), ML 12, AL Chaotic Evil, XP 50, NA 2d4 (1d8+2), TT B, Abilities: Undead and Plant Vulnerability, Physical Immunity , Silent Killer, Sense Living (90'), Infectious Touch (drain 1d6 CON), Unimpeded

---

Firing the Cannon

If the party decides to try and fire the cannon from this area (the base of the tower), they have a -3 to hit as they don't have enough height.

Pirate Landfall

When it's time for Vocini's crew to make landfall (see *Structure of the Adventure - Part 4 Pirate Landfall*), the mages aboard the ship use their *Staves of Travel* (see *Magical Items*) to send crew through portals to Area 7 and here, Area 10.

Every round the portals are open, three Basic Pirates and two Tough Pirates (see *Creatures*) arrive in Area 7 and in Area 10. If the pirates are unaware of the party (no firing of the cannon, no noticed on the shoreline), then the pirates split up to secure Area 4, Area 6, and the tower. After 10 rounds of pirates making landfall, Vocini joins them to hunt for the *Cannon of the Blessed*.

Aiding the staff-wielding mages is a Tough Pirate with a spyglass, keeping an eye on what's happening on shore and giving advice, such as moving the portals, closing them, etc. The pirate has a 1-in-6 chance of noticing any party members out in the open per minute.

10A - Bottom of the Tower

Entering the bottom of the tower, you notice it has a mix of fancy, exquisite tile of irregular shapes with common stone shoved in to replace broken or ripped out ones. It looks like it was built by an artist and repaired by brutes.

The grey plaster of the walls has peeled in many places or is missing completely, revealing the stone of the outer wall. There are a few rectangular areas of discoloration on the plaster, as if paintings or something had been in place for a long time. There are four hooks on the walls spread out evenly, perhaps for lanterns.

On the far side from the entrance appears to be a mound of broken furniture and refuse covered in a sheen of swamp slime. You can see what appears to be the remains of once fancy chairs, a broken dresser, a bookcase, and a desk.

In the middle of the tower is a spiral staircase, also covered in swamp slime. Its stone steps are so worn in the middle as to be half the height they were originally. In the walls of the staircase are arrowheads and pieces of blades from battles long forgotten.

GM's Notes

Hidden in the furniture

Under the toppled dresser can be found the skeleton of someone dressed in decayed pirate garb.

Stuffed in the skull's mouth is a well-preserved letter that appears to be a signet-signed deal from an unfamiliar nation offering 50,000gp and passage away from the peninsula in exchange for the *Cannon of the Blessed* and elimination of all those remaining at the outpost.

Slippery stairs

The stairs are very slick. Anyone with a dexterity of 11 and above may walk up them slowly, without issue. Otherwise, a dexterity check is necessary every floor. Failure results in falling down a flight of stairs to the lower level and taking 1d6 damage.

10b - Middle floor of the Tower

What was likely once a great room has the wind ripping through its holes in the outer wall, floor, and ceiling. Weathered, dark-green, drapes billow gently with the sea breeze, distracting from the missing floor-to-ceiling section of the wall and pieces of the slick floor.

Some chunks of grey plaster remains on the interior walls, and the floor here is also covered in a veneer of slippery goo. Scattered about the floor are piles of debris from the caved-in ceiling. A large, discolored rectangular area suggests a rug may have once been, some of its details having seeped into the tiles. There are several small puddles. Looking up in some areas, you can see through the top floor to the dark clouds above.

On the eastern wall hangs something on the wall covered in a stained, heavy sheet. It is approximately four feet wide by three feet tall. The sheet is pinned in place by two rusted daggers. The bottom of the sheet gently dances with the wind.

GM's Notes

Drapes

The thick drapes are clutching to a thick, tarnished silver rod (worth 200gp). The drapes are made up of a pattern of one foot by one foot patches. One of said patches is actually a secret pocket with a *Scroll of Feather Fall* – probably someone's emergency escape plan that was never used.

Dagger, sheet, and the painting

Lifting the sheet reveals a painting showing that very room, though in much better condition. It shows several skeletons in the room. The painted window shows no other buildings.

If the daggers are removed, then the protective spell is broken and the painting comes to life. Everyone looking at it must make a Save vs Spells (wisdom) or be sucked into the painting where they are trapped in the room, unable to leave it.

Anyone trapped in the dimensional pocket of the painting is unable to hear the voices in the real world, and vice-versa. However, they are each able to see each other in the painting.

On the back of the frame is an engraved magical word in both the real world and the pocket dimension, though different ones in each. Each word needs to be said aloud, which frees those trapped in the painting.

The entrapment magic only works once per day.

If the painting is removed from the tower, it stops working. If a character is trapped in the painting when that happens, they are stuck in the pocket dimension unable to see the real world and vice versa.

Superior place to fire

If the party has not found the note that indicated the second floor is the best place to fire the cannon from, allow any character with an intelligence 13+, or wisdom 13+, to make a check. If they succeed, they have a feeling that firing the cannon, and watching from behind the traps, might be better than the roof. Firing from here gives an additional +2 to hit.

As a reminder, when *Part 4 - Landfall* (see *Structure of the Adventure*) happens, and the pirate ship is 240 feet away, it can

be fired upon. The ship has an AC 4 [15], and the party needs to do 60 points of damage to sink it before the pirates make landfall.

Climbing the stairs

If the party is carrying the cannon barrel, or anything else heavy and awkward, they need to make a dexterity check. Failing results in taking 1d6 damage per floor, with another roll needed for the next floor.

10c - Top of the Tower

The last few stairs up to the top of the tower are in shambles. The stones are broken and wobbly, and everything is covered in slick, jellied swamp slime.

The stone parapets that once would have provided a protective edge around the top of the tower are little more than a memory, with most of the third floor's defenses looking like they had been smashed away by a raging giant. Large chunks of the floor are also missing, as if having been cleaved away.

Still, from up here you have a clear view over the entire area and out to sea. You can imagine a lookout scanning the horizon for pirates or a wizard calling out to creatures of the sea.

The recommendation had been to fire the cannon from as close to the edge of the top of the tower as possible, but getting there is clearly going to be dangerous.

GM's Notes
Firing at will

If the party decides to fire the cannon from the top of the tower, they have no bonus or penalty to hit the ship. As a reminder, the ship has an AC 4 [15] and 60 HP.

Every time the cannon is fired from the top of the tower, there's a 2-in-6 it starts to slip. A strength check is needed to prevent it from either falling down to the second floor or falling off the tower entirely (GM's choice). If multiple characters are immediately beside the cannon when it slips, use the highest strength for the check and give a +1 bonus to per character helping (see *Ability Checks and Difficulty*).

Map 2 - Underground

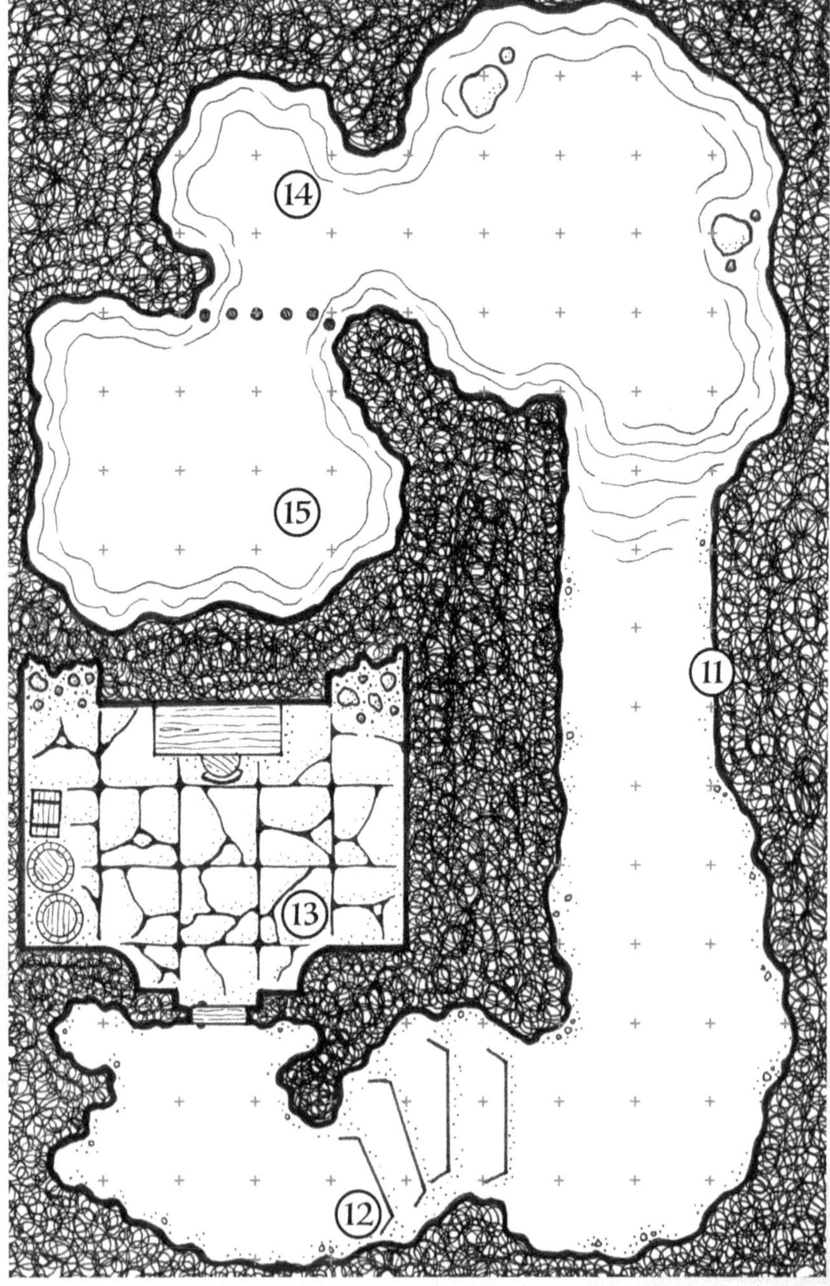

Areas - Underground

As you descend the rickety ladder into the darkness, humidity and dankness envelops the party and assaults you with the smell of rotting plant life. You descend the ladder slowly, finding it becomes more slippery the further down you go.

Arriving at the bottom of the ladder, you can't see anything. A chill washes over you as you get to the bottom, leaving behind a sense of anger and sadness.

At the bottom of the ladder is swamp water and not floor. You can't tell how deep it is.

GM's Notes

Darkness and infravision

The underground area seems to absorb light, reducing the effectiveness of torches, lanterns, and other light sources by half.

The swamp fog screws with infravision, making it appear that there are illusionary heat and cold images that come and go.

Surroundings and the water

Illuminating the surroundings reveals a tunnel extending north and south consumed by the swamp. Vines and greenery coat the walls and ceiling. Skeletal faces appear embedded in the walls, covered in moss or slime.

The swamp water is two feet deep and quickly penetrates non-magical boots, clothing, and armor irritating the skin. It's depth slows movement.

- **Medium-sized**. Movement is reduced by 50%, and they have a -2 to AC.
- **Small-sized**. Movement is reduced by 75%, and they have a -3 to AC.

Returning to the location

If the party returns to Area 11 without having freed the Sea Witch, they are ambushed by 2d4 Swamp Wights clinging to the walls and ceiling.

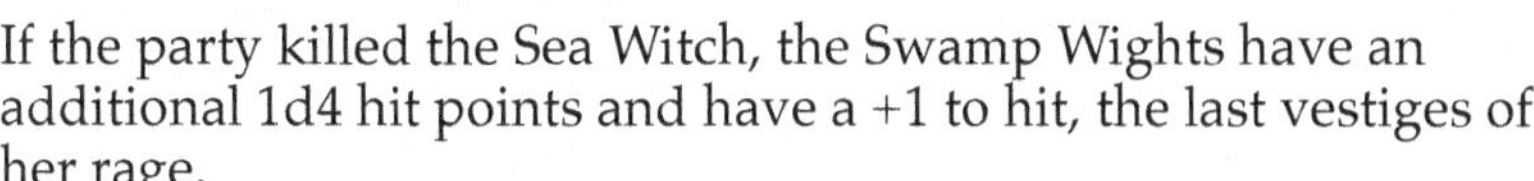

If the party killed the Sea Witch, the Swamp Wights have an additional 1d4 hit points and have a +1 to hit, the last vestiges of her rage.

If she was released, the Swamp Wights won't appear.

> **Swamp Wights**
>
> *AC 5 [14], HD 3 (13 HP), Att 1x claws (1d8) or infectious touch, THAC0 17 [+2], MV 120' (40'), SV D12 W13 P14 B15 S16 (3), ML 12, AL Chaotic Evil, XP 50, NA 2d4 (1d8+2),TT B, Abilities: Undead and Plant Vulnerability, Physical Immunity , Silent Killer, Sense Living (90'), Infectious Touch (drain 1d6 CON), Unimpeded*

12 - ALCOVES AND STAIRS

As you come around the corner, you can feel there are steps hidden under the swamp water. The wide tunnel turns northward, where a large wooden door with black metal braces to reinforce it sits above the swamp water line. There are three shadow alcoves: two on the western side, one on the eastern.

Lurking

Hiding in each of the alcoves is one Swamp Wight, while under the water are two Swamp Zomtrees.

If the party hasn't freed the Sea Witch, then they wait until the party is in the middle of the area and then attack from all sides.

If the party did free the Sea Witch, they do nothing, content with leaving the party alone unless attacked.

> **Swamp Wights**
>
> *AC 5 [14], HD 3 (13 HP), Att 1x claws (1d8) or infectious touch, THAC0 17 [+2], MV 120' (40'), SV D12 W13 P14 B15 S16 (3), ML 12, AL Chaotic Evil, XP 50, NA 2d4 (1d8+2),TT B, Abilities: Undead and Plant Vulnerability, Physical Immunity, Silent Killer, Sense Living (90'), Infectious Touch (drain 1d6 CON), Unimpeded*
>
> **Swamp Zomtrees**
>
> *AC 2 [17], HD 7 (32 HP), Att 2x branch claws (2d6 each), THAC0 12 [+7], MV 60' (20'), SV D8 W9 P10 B10 S12 (8), ML 9, AL Chaotic Evil, XP 650, NA 1d4 (1d8), TT C, Abilities: Unholy Scream, Undead and Plant Vulnerabilities, Immunity, Camouflage, Extended Reach*

Door and Lock

The door has a metal handle and is locked. It has many deep scratches in it. The lock on the door is a sophisticated double lock, requiring two successful pick attempts. Failing to pick the lock results in a shock for 2d6 damage. Failing to pick the second one results in the first lock resetting and requiring the player to start over.

Attempting to bash down the door is equally challenging. If you're using a Bash-Doors d6 type of system, use a d12 instead (thus a 3-in-6 becomes a 3-in-12) and apply a -1 penalty to the attempt. With each attempt, the player receives a shock for 2d6 damage. After two successful bashing attempts in a row, the door swings open.

Treasure in an Alcove

Hidden in one of the alcoves on a shelf carved into the cave wall is a *Buckler +2* and a *Wand of Magic Missiles* (10 charges). They are wrapped in brown leather and hard to see from a distance. It feels like this was someone's personal cache, but there's no indication of whom.

13 - OFFICE

You see a partially caved-in storage room and office, and you smell a mix of ash and stale beer. The stone floor is unexpectedly free of slime and swamp water. Laying in the middle of the room are bones and a pile of ash, like a makeshift campfire. The walls have black smoke stains.

There are four large barrels stacked up against the western wall. Beside them are a stack of wooden crates.

Against the northern wall, flanked by caved-in passages, is a simple looking desk and chair. The desk is covered in a messy array of papers and assortment of ink bottles. On the wall in front of the desk is a hand-drawn map of the area with markings on it.

On the eastern wall is a shelf and large wooden pegs with two coils of rope and a dented shield. On the shelf are a half-dozen lanterns. Hiding in the shadows below it are blood-stained bedrolls and blankets.

GM's Notes

Skeletons

Three of the skeletons have skulls that have been bashed in from behind. One is missing an arm and another is missing a leg. Close examination reveals four of the skeletons have bite marks on the arms and legs. The last one doesn't show any wounds.

Crates

There are five empty crates stacked up. Judging by the writing on them, they were likely once used for transporting fruits and vegetables.

Map

The map is of the surrounding area and likely from a long time ago. There is a circle around Area 3, with word: pickup.

Special Barrel

One of the barrels is magical and has parts of what look like two decomposed bodies in it. The barrel is *Arfon's Barrel of Bedlam* (see *Magical Items*). The bodies have bite marks and are missing limbs. It also contains stale feces.

Caved-in sections

There are skeletal remains poking out, indicating that it took people by surprise. There's no way to get past the cave-in.

Lanterns and rope

If a successful *Find Traps* attempt is made on the shelf or lanterns, the character notices three of the six lanterns have been tampered with and are likely to burst into flames after several minutes of use (1d20), resulting in 1d4 damage and igniting anything flammable in the immediate area.

The ropes are made of hemp and 30 feet long. Close inspection shows lots of little bite marks, as if someone was so hungry they kept trying to see if they could eat it. The rope is unreliable if used to hold more than a hundred pounds (4-in-6 chance of breaking every minute).

Desk

On the desk are some papers with faded dates showing what was shipping in and out of the fort. It appears that the outpost captain had a smuggling side-business and was working with the traitorous crew for years without McFinly knowing.

Potential Rest Spot

Though time is of the essence, the party may decide to rest, or even try to wait out Vocini, here. This area is ideal. The door can be easily locked safely from the inside, and the pirates won't enter the room.

14 - Columns of Sorrow

As you make your way through the tunnel, the swamp water becomes ever thicker, lightly burning exposed skin. There are plants growing out of the swampy water, going up to the ceiling. Flowering vines cling to the walls. Purple glowing moss randomly scattered about, providing just enough light to set an eerie and foreboding scene.

Up ahead is a series of thick columns wrapped in vines and set about a foot apart from each other. The columns block your path. Beyond them is overgrown vegetation, and you can hear water falling somewhere ahead. You feel a presence notice you.

GM's Notes

Columns

Hidden underneath the vines and greenery of the columns are corroded, thick metal bars and a jail door. The jail door's lock cannot be picked and needs to be forced open (strength check). Destroying a column requires 30 HP of damage.

The bars go deep into the ceiling and the floor.

Call for help

The party feels the presence of the Sea Witch in their minds. They sense tremendous injustice, rage, and a demand to be set free.

Leaving the Sea Witch

If the party goes through to Area 15, only to return without having freed the Sea Witch, then there are 2d4 Swamp Wights waiting for the party.

If the party killed the Sea Witch, the Swamp Wights have an additional 1d4 hit points and have a +1 to hit, the last vestiges of her rage.

Swamp Wights

AC 5 [14], HD 3 (13 HP), Att 1x claws (1d8) or infectious touch, THAC0 17 [+2], MV 120' (40'), SV D12 W13 P14 B15 S16 (3), ML 12, AL Chaotic Evil, XP 50, NA 2d4 (1d8+2),TT B, Abilities: Undead and Plant Vulnerability, Physical Immunity, Silent Killer, Sense Living (90'), Infectious Touch (drain 1d6 CON), Unimpeded

---

15 - SEA WITCH

As you enter this area, you feel it crowded with vegetation. High above, the jagged tunnel ceiling is covered in a silvery luminescent mold, and swamp water is pouring in like waterfalls.

Slowly, the vegetation pulls back, revealing an emaciated figure covered in swamp plants and chained to the back wall. It stirs, its eyes glowing a golden yellow.

Your minds are flooded with images. You see a pirate ship coming toward the shore, its captain slain. You see a woman aboard, in pale blue wizard robes and chained up, her fingers broken. As the ship makes land, there's an argument between the first-mate-turned-mutineer captain and the quartermaster about letting the mage go free. The quartermaster is slain and thrown into the sea. "The Sea Witch isn't going anywhere. McFinly's going to pay handsomely for her and the cannon," echoes in the room.

The scene jumps to several months later as the outpost's captain decides to try and change the deal with the pirates, who have helped keep any forces at bay with the *Cannon of the Blessed*. "McFinly's dead, we have the cannon. Let the witch go. She's not worth the trouble." The words go unheeded. The Sea Witch

attempts to escape twice, only to be beaten and then jailed underground.

Weeks later, a drunk soldier filled with guilt goes to taunt the Sea Witch, telling her of McFinly's death and unlocking her rage. The area is taken over by a swamp and filled with strange creatures. The soldiers and crew try to hold the outpost, but eventually they fall.

Time skips ahead years and years. The curious come to the outpost and are killed, adventures come and go. Finally there is nothing but quiet as she is forgotten entirely, bound with magical chains.

Your minds return to the present, and you feel the twinkling eyes of the Sea Witch staring into your souls. You hear words in your minds: "Free me."

GM's Notes

Sea Witch

The Sea Witch is magically chained to the wall by her forearms. Her skin is a dark green and black. Her eyes shine like emeralds.

The chains are about to fail, though she doesn't know. Their magic has slowly leaked away. Should the party attack her, the chains suddenly give way as she tries to dodge a blow. If an attack misses, it breaks the chains frees her.

Her mind is damaged, making her telepathic communication potentially overwhelming. If the party debates what to do, she grows impatient and can summon four Swamp Zomtrees out of the surrounding swamp greenery to attack. She would rather die than remain imprisoned.

Swamp Zomtrees

AC 2 [17], HD 7 (32 HP), Att 2x branch claws (2d6 each), THAC0 12 [+7], MV 60' (20'), SV D8 W9 P10 B10 S12 (8), ML 9, AL Chaotic Evil, XP 650, NA 1d4 (1d8), TT C, Abilities: Unholy Scream, Undead and Plant Vulnerabilities, Immunity, Camouflage, Extended Reach

---

Sea Witch - Freed

If the party frees her before the pirate ship makes landfall, then the Sea Witch creates 5 Swamp Wights who will protect the party. She will send an image of protection into minds of each member of the party. If the party attacks them, the directive to protect the party is gone, and they attack back.

Before the party goes, she puts the image of a secret nook in Area 14 where there's a *Hilt of the Discerning* (see *Magical Items*) with a *Short Sword of the Flame* (see *Magical Items*) in it.

Sea Witch - Abandoned

If the party decides to leave the Sea Witch chained up, she becomes absolutely furious. All encounters from her prison to the tower have the maximum number of creatures (e.g. 2d4 would result in 8), have 4 additional hit points, and are hostile. She will free herself within an hour and then seeks to destroy all trespassers in the area.

Sea Witch - Attacked

If the party attacks the Sea Witch, she becomes furious. Her rage and grief at being left there pushes her over the edge.

The vines on the walls become alive and attempt to entangle any party member within the room each round, requiring a saving throw versus paralysis. Adventurers entangled by the vines suffer a -3 penalty to hit, -3 penalty to their AC, and can't cast spells. She also summons the Swamp Zomtrees mentioned earlier.

Sea Witch

AC: 1 [18], HD6+2 (30 HP), Att Overwhelm or 2x Claws (2d8 each), THAC0 15 [+4], MV 120'(40'), SV D10, W11, P12, B13, S14 (6), ML 10, AL Chaotic Neutral, XP 550

- **Overwhelm.** She is able to instill fear in one target. Save versus Paralysis or suffer -2 AC, -2 to attack, and be unable to cast for 1d4+2 rounds.

The End

There are a few likely endings and one potential twist ending.

Mission accomplished

The party found all of the parts of the *Cannon of the Blessed*, sank Vocini's ship, and arrives back at Area 1 for their pick up before the midnight deadline. Everyone gets into the coaches, strapping down gear on the roof then heading back to the capital city for ceremonies, feasting, and receiving rewards and accolades.

Potential twist

The ride back to the city is cut short as Vocini's contingency plan is activated. The coaches are ambushed by 50 Tough Pirates and 2 mages. They were from a second ship with a simple plan: capture the cannon at all costs and make the capital city pay.

Reward

For returning the cannon, the party is to rewarded with 20,000gp and one of the following magical items for each surviving member of the party:

- *20 Arrows of the Melee Master +2 (see Magical Items)*
- *Cloak of Protection +2, +3 vs Undead*
- *Gloves of Dexterity*
- *Plate Mail +2, +3 vs Undead*
- *Ring of Regeneration*
- *Ring of Spell Storing*
- *Scroll Case of Power (see Magical Items)*
- *Two-handed Sword +2, +4 vs plants and plant-based creatures*

Reward for the Returned Halberd

Yokik had offered a reward for finding and returning the *Halberd of the Storm*. She pays 25,000gp and gives a *Shrinking Spear of Wounding (see Magical Items)*.

EMPTY HANDED

The party arrives at Area 1 without the cannon before the pickup deadline passes, whether fleeing Vocini's forces or having dispatched them. Yokik convinces the grand magistrate that they should reveal themselves to the party and discern what has happened, before putting a bounty on the heads of the party.

VOCINI'S UPPER HAND

For whatever reason, the *Cannon of the Blessed* has fallen into the hands of the now future pirate king, Vocini. Perhaps his forces overwhelmed the party or perhaps his forces found the parts of the cannon first. Regardless, the grand magistrate sees this as the worst form of failure, or even treason, and abandons the party leaving only a note stuck to a tree with a knife. The note is a wanted poster with the names of the party and a 50,000gp reward for their dead bodies.

The party must either escape the peninsula or clear their names.

CANNON IS THE THING

The party missed the pickup window but have the cannon. Perhaps they managed to defeat Vocini's landed troops, or they hid long enough that Vocini left empty-handed. After hauling the cannon back to the capital city on their own, and being granted an audience with the grand magistrate, the party receives half their monetary reward as word has already been sent that the mission failed.

Potential twist

Vocini's spies, or others interested in the *Cannon of the Blessed*, try to convince the party to sell them the cannon as their efforts have not been appreciated. If they do, havoc is wreaked upon the city with the names of the heroes used to make it seem like they are the ones provoking the action.

REVENGE

The party arrives to find the coaches destroyed, the grand magistrate dead, and swamp slime everywhere. Only a golden eyed Yokik remains. Perhaps the Sea Witch did this after the party was dropped off, or after they freed her, or just before she died. She now possesses Yokik and leads the party back to town where she'll take control of the cannon, kill the chancellor, and seek to rule.

Checks, Stats, and More

If you're not yet familiar with ability checks or with creature stat blocks (aka statistic blocks), or would like a review them, then read on.

Ability Checks and Difficulty

There are points in this adventure where an ability check is recommended to see if something happens to a character, such as they slip on slick rocks and fall into the river. Most old school RPGs use one of two game mechanics for ability checks:

- Roll under their as used in *Old-School Essentials*, *B/X* and *1e*
- Roll over a target number, often called a Difficulty Class (DC).

Encounters may state a particular ability check is *hard* or *easy*. If the encounter doesn't state a particular difficulty, then it is assumed to be *medium*. In order to keep this adventure cross-compatible, a table of modifiers is listed below.

Difficulty	Target or bonus/penalty to attempt
Easy	*DC8 or +2 bonus*
Medium	*DC12 or no bonus/penalty*
Hard	*DC16 or -2 penalty*
Very Hard	*DC20 or -4 penalty*

Creature Stat Blocks

Each encounter that has creatures includes a summary stat block in an *Old-School Essentials* inspired style. This provides the essential information as to what the creature's armor class is, how many attacks it has, how much damage it can do, the list of special abilities it may have, and more. Details about any particular abilities the creature possesses will usually found at the back of the adventure in the *Creatures* section, rather than repeating them for every encounter the creature appears in.

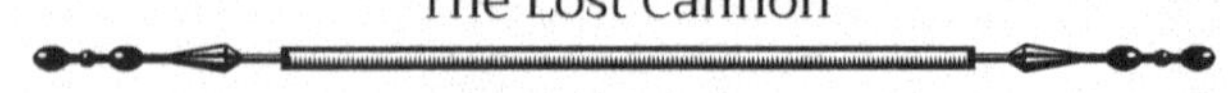

> **Crazed Bandit**
>
> *AC 6 [14], HD 3+1 (13 HP), Att 1x Short Sword (1d6), MV 120'*
> *(40'), THAC0 18 [+1], SV D13 W14 P13 B16 S15 (Thief 1), ML 8,*
> *AL Neutral Evil, XP 10, NA 1d8 (3d10), TT U, Abilities: A, B, C*
>
> *Items:*
>
> - Item 1
> - Item 2

Here's an example stat block with explanations for each part:

AC 6 [14] There are two Armor Class values provided. The first number shown (6) is the classic Descending AC used with lookup attack tables. The second is for systems using Ascending AC (AAC).

HD 3+1 (13 HP) This is the creature's Hit Dice, representing what level it is and how many eight-sided dice (d8) it has of potential hit points. If there is an additional number, like the +1 in this case, that's the number of additional hit points added to the total. The hit points for the creature can be rolled or you can use the number provided in parentheses.

Att 1x Short Sword (1d6) Attack shows how many attacks the creature has per round as well as the type of weapon it uses and the damage its weapon does. In this example, the creature has one attack per round and uses a sword, rather than claws or a bite, and the sword attack does 1d6 damage per hit.

MV 120' (40') Movement has two numbers. The first (120') is how many feet the creature can move as its base movement rate. The second (40') shows the number of feet the creature can move, on its turn, in combat. In general, the base movement rate is 3x the encounter rate.

THAC0 18 [+1] This is To-Hit-Armor-Class-Zero, or THAC0. The first number shown, 18, is used with Descending Armor Class and shows what the creature would need to hit an AC 0. If the creature were attacking a player with a Descending AC of 3, then they would need a 15. The number in brackets is used with AAC and shows the bonus to the die the creature gets when rolling to attack.

If the player has an AAC 15, then the creature rolls a d20 and adds +1 to their die roll.

SV D13 W14 P13 B16 S15 (Thief 1) These are the creature's saving throws. D is for the death/poison saving throw, W is for wand, P for paralysis/petrification, B for breath weapon, and S for spell. If you want to use the classic saving throw charts, use the information in parentheses. In this case, it shows a level 1 thief. If no class is specified, then it means it is using the monster entry on the saving throw table.

ML 8 This is the creature's morale rating, which determines if a creature is going to flee or stand and fight.

Al Neutral Evil This is the creature's alignment. If you are playing a B/X style game, like *Old-School Essentials Basic*, ignore the Evil/Good part of the alignment.

XP 10 This shows how many experience points (XP) besting a single creature of this type is worth. That could mean killing them, sneaking past them, etc., as determined by the GM.

NA 1d8 (3d10) Number Appearing shows you how many you are likely to find wandering around, in this case 1d8. The number in the parentheses shows how many would be found in a lair, encampment, or group. In this example, that'd be 3d10.

TT U (A) This tells you what treasure table to use from the GM's guide, like the *Old-School Essentials Advanced Fantasy Referee's Tome* or the *Treasure* book from the *Old-School Essentials Classic Game Set*. The first letter, U, indicates what treasure table to use for an individual creature. The letter in parentheses, A, identifies the treasure table to be used for a lair or encampment. Note that this is only used in the adventure in the case of a random encounter.

Abilities: The abilities section summarizes any special abilities the creatures have. In a particular encounter, if the creature is unique to that one encounter, then the description of the abilities are listed below. However, if the creature appears in multiple encounters, or could be a random encounter, only the names of the abilities are included in the encounter with the details provided in the *Creatures* section of this adventure.

Items: If the creature has magical items, they are listed in bullets after the stat block. If the creature has a magical item, like a *Club +1* or a *Shield +2*, the associated bonuses for those items have not been applied to the creature's stats (like to hit or AC). The GM needs to add them. The reason for this is because the creature could be relieved of these items through many clever means.

Creatures

Crocodile, Large

These large reptiles are approximately 20 feet long and patrol the ancient ruins, attacking or scaring off those that the Sea-Witch wouldn't want there.

AC 3 [16], HD 6 (25 HP), Att 1x bite (2d8), THAC0 14 [+5], MV 90' (30') / 90' (30') swimming, SV D12 W13 P14 B15 S16 (3), ML 7, AL Neutral, XP 275, NA 0 (1d4), TT None

Swamp Wight

These creatures look like humanoids covered in green and black ooze, often with plants growing on them or out of them. They are a strange mix of undead and plant life, with no memory of who they were. To many they can seem like zombies, moving slowly. However, once there is something of interest to them, they move quickly and in packs.

AC 5 [14], HD 3 (13 HP), Att 1x claws (1d8) or infectious touch, THAC0 17 [+2], MV 120' (40'), SV D12 W13 P14 B15 S16 (3), ML 12, AL Chaotic Evil, XP 50, NA 2d4 (1d8+2),TT B

- *Undead and Plant Vulnerability.* Swamp Wights are affected by magic that affects either undead or plants. Holy water causes 1d4 damage (unless otherwise specified). A successful *Turn Undead* against them only results in them having a -2 to hit and a -2 to AC for 1d4 rounds instead of making them flee or destroying them.

- *Physical Immunity.* They are immune to poison, disease, sleep, charm, hold, mind-affecting magic, and mind-reading magic. They are also immune to non-magical and silver weapons. They have a vulnerability to weapons with copper coatings.

- *Silent Killer.* These creatures make no noise when they move or attack. They are able to communicate with other Swamp Wights within 120 feet.

- *Sense Living.* Swamp Wights can sense living creatures within 90 feet and work in packs.

- *Infectious Touch.* They can attempt to lay a hand on an opponent (a touch attack). If successful, it drains the target of 1d6 constitution points for 1 hour (update hit points appropriately). If the target's constitution drops to 2 or below, they become a Swamp Wight immediately.

- *Unimpeded*. Swamp Wights are able to move at full speed in up to thigh-high swamps, water hazards, and the like.

SWAMP SPECTER

These ghostly creatures usually look like an ethereal, decayed person with plants growing out of them. Some can be found to be relatively harmless if left alone, mentally lost and mumbling, trying to make sense of their fate. Others can be found protecting something, patrolling around, looking for any that could threaten that which they have sworn to protect.

*AC 0 [19], HD 10** (45 HP), Att 1 touch (life drain) or 2x spectral claws (2d6 each), THAC0 11 [+8], MV 90' (30'), SV D6 W7 P8 B8 S10 (10), ML 10, AL Any, XP 2750, TT E, N*

- *Undead and Plant Vulnerability*. Swamp Specters are affected by magic that affects either undead or plants. Holy water causes 1d4 damage (unless otherwise specified) and a successful *Turn Undead* against them only results in them having a -2 to hit and a -2 to AC for 4 rounds instead of making them flee or destroying them.

- *Physical Immunity*. They are immune to poison, disease, sleep, charm, hold, mind-affecting and mind-reading magic. They are also immune to non-magical and silver weapons. They have a vulnerability to weapons with copper coatings.

- *Fright*. They are able to perform a fear attack causing all those who can see them (within 30 feet) to Save vs Paralysis or be struck with fear and unable to move for 1d4 rounds.

- *Life drain*. This touch-attack causes the victim to lose 1d4 points of constitution and heals the Swamp Specter 1d4 per point drained. If the victim hits a constitution of zero, they die and are unable to be raised from the dead except by a wish.

- *Spectral claws*. The Swamp Specter is able to use their sharp spectral fingers as weapons (2d6 damage each). A successful attack requires a Save vs Death or suffer 1 point of constitution loss (heal 1 con/day)

SWAMP ZOMTREE

These creatures appear like swamp-covered treefolk with the bodies of humanoids embedded in them. They are usually 8 to 10 feet tall and several feet wide, though some are shorter and wider.

AC 2 [17], HD 7 (32 HP), Att 2x branch claws (2d6 each), THAC0 12 [+7], MV 60' (20'), SV D8 W9 P10 B10 S12 (8), ML 9, AL Chaotic Evil, XP 650, NA 1d4 (1d8), TT C

- *Unholy Scream.* Instead of a standard attack, they can make all the mouths on their bodies emit a horrifying scream affecting any living creature within 90 feet. Save vs Death or take 1d8+1 damage and be stunned for 1d4 rounds.

- *Undead and Plant Vulnerabilities.* Swamp Zomtrees are affected by magic that affects either undead or plants. Holy water causes 1d4 damage (unless otherwise specified). A successful *Turn Undead* against them only results in them having a -2 to hit and a -2 to AC for 1d4 rounds instead of making them flee or destroying them.

- *Immunity.* They are immune to poison, disease, sleep, charm, hold, mind-affecting magic, and mind-reading magic. They are also immune to non-magical and silver weapons. They have a vulnerability to weapons with copper coatings.

- *Camouflage.* Swamp Zomtrees are able to appear as normal swamp plants and often wait for unsuspecting prey to move within striking range and then surprise them. When remaining still, they are indistinguishable from regular swamp foliage.

- *Extended Reach.* They are able to attack opponents up to 15 feet away.

Swamp Zomtree, Giant

Though not as common as the Swamp Zomtree, these giant versions are far more deadly. They stand 12-15 feet high and tend to have four branches they can use as arms to attack.

AC 1 [18], HD 8 (40 HP), Att 4x branch claws (2d6 each), THAC0 12 [+7], MV 60' (20'), SV D8 W9 P10 B10 S12 (8), ML 9, AL Chaotic Evil, XP 750

- *Entangle.* The legs of a giant Swamp Zomtree have tendrils that try to grab any opponent within 5 feet (typical melee weapon range). The opponent must make a Save vs Paralysis or become entangled (they can try to break away every round). One giant Swamp Zomtree can have up to two entangled opponents at one time.

- *Undead and Plant Vulnerability.* Giant Swamp Zomtrees are affected by magic that affects either undead or plants. Holy water causes 1d4 damage (unless otherwise specified). A successful *Turn Undead* against them only results in them having a -2 to hit and a -2 to AC for 1d4 rounds instead of making them flee or destroying them.

- *Immunity.* They are immune to poison, disease, sleep, charm, hold, mind-affecting magic, and mind-reading magic. They are also immune to non-magical and silver weapons. They have a vulnerability to weapons with copper coatings.

- *Camouflage.* Giant Swamp Zomtrees are able to appear as normal swamp trees, including reducing their height by up to 50%. They often wait for unsuspecting prey to move within striking range and

then surprise them. When remaining still, they are indistinguishable from regular swamp foliage.

- *Swamp Portal.* They have the ability to sink into the swamp and emerge anywhere else in the swamp, up to 240 feet away. They can use this ability up to 3x per day and generally use it to escape.

- *Extended Reach.* They are able to attack opponents up to 20 feet away.

Vocini and Crew

The party's not intended to encounter the pirate lord and his crew, but great adventures have a tendency to take unexpected turns. The description of what happens during *Part 4 - Pirate Landfall* is presented at the end of this section.

Vocini

Vocini is a smart, ruthless pirate who is determined to break the navy of the peninsula and then take it over in its entirety.

He's deft with a sword and his wit. It's said he's convinced as many to join him with words as the edge of his blade. He inspires loyalty from others, but is only loyal to very few.

If hard pressed, Vocini flees using his *Boots of Water Walking* to run away.

He is singularly focused on getting the *Cannon of the Blessed* and is intimately knowledgeable of what it looks like and how it works, as he has been researching it for years.

7th level Fighter. Str: 16, Int: 15, Wis: 9, Dex: 15, Con: 11, Cha: 16. AC 4 [15], HD 7 (34 HP), THAC0 14 [+5], MV 90' (30'), SV D:8 W:9 P:10 B:11 S:12 (Fighter 7), AL Neutral Evil, XP 750

- He has a *Cutlass of the Seas* (+1 to hit, +2 damage on land, +2 to hit and +3 damage when in or on water, see *Magical Items*)

- *Leather Armor +2*

- *Boots of Water Walking* (see *Magical Items*)

- 2 *Potions of Cure Serious Wounds* (2d6+2)

- He has a medallion worth 1000gp on him that has high sentimental value to him. It was his father's (could be used as a plot hook for claiming the chancellorship).

Pirate Ship

The ship itself has an AC 4 [15] and 40 HP, is immune to normal attacks by the party. Magical attacks against the ship only do ¼ damage. Attacks from the *Cannon of the Blessed*, other cannons, and giant weapons do full damage.

Pirate Crew

Vocini has a crew made up of:

- 3 Pirate Mages
- 40 Tough Pirates
- 60 Basic Pirates

Basic Pirates

These eager, young pirates are thrown at opponents to wear them down or overwhelm them. They are reasonably well-armed for pirates. Each one has leather armor, a cutlass (short sword), and a dagger. Each one has a few coins on them (1d10 gp, 1d10 sp).

AC 5 [14], HD 1 (4 HP), Att 1x weapon (1d6 light crossbow or cutlass), THAC0 19 [0], MV 120' (40'), SV D12 W13 P14 B15 S16 (1), ML 7, AL Chaotic Neutral, XP 10

Tough Pirates

They are very well armed, having short bows (8 arrows each, +1 to hit due to high dexterity), superior cutlasses (+1 to hit and damage), and light chainmail (half-weight).

They coordinate their attacks on spellcasters and those wearing robes first.

AC 3 [16], HD 2 (12 HP), Att 1x weapon (1d6+1 cutlass, 1d8 bow), THAC0 17 [+2], MV 120' (40'), SV D11 W12 P13 B14 S15 (2), ML 9, AL Neutral Evil, XP 15

Pirate Mages

If Vocini is leaving the ship, then one pirate mage may go with him, otherwise the pirate mages remain on the ship. They are third-level magical spellcasters and are fiercely loyal to Vocini. If the ship is sinking, they will abandon it however.

5th level Magic-User, AC 6 [13], HD 5 (10 HP), Att 1x Spell or dagger (1d4), THAC0 19 [0], MV 120' (40'), SV D13 W14 P13 B16 S15, ML 8, AL Neutral Evil, XP 360

- *Robes.* Each of the pirate mages are wearing Robes of Protection which grants them AC 6 [13] and absorbs 1 point of damage per round.

- *Spells.* They are able to cast *Magic Missile* (twice), *Enhanced Magic Missile* (twice) which is a second level version of *Magic Missile* able to be used on two targets that are within 60′ of each other, and they have *Hold Person* (once).

- *Wand of Fireballs.* While two of the pirate mages are wielding a *Staff of Travel* (see *Magical Items)*, the third mage wields a *Wand of Fireballs* with 5 charges in it. It can be used to fire at targets up to 240 feet away and delivers 6d6 damage to anyone within 30 feet of the targeted area (Save vs Breath Weapon for half).

Landfall

When it's time for the pirates to make landfall (see *Structure of the Adventure - Part 4 Pirate Landfall)*, two portals are opened from Vocini's ship: one to Area 7 and the other to Area 10. If the ship is hit by the *Cannon of the Blessed* while the portals are open, the mages close the portals for 1d4 rounds before reopening them.

Every round the portals are open, three Basic Pirates and two Tough Pirates arrive in Area 7 and in Area 10. If the pirates are unaware of the party (no firing of the cannon, no one visible on the shoreline), then they split up to secure Area 4, Area 6, and the tower. After 10 rounds of pirates making landfall, Vocini joins them, and they hunt for the cannon.

If the pirates are aware of the party, then the pirates rush the party, potentially moving the location of one of the portals behind the party's location. In this scenario, the pirates continue landfall for 15 rounds (instead of 10), after which Vocini joins them with a pirate mage to finish the battle with the party.

Potential Outcomes

Vocini is a tactician. He will sacrifice his crew if it is clear he is losing, or he will strike a bargain with the party. He has more than 100,000gp worth of coins, jewels, and trinkets aboard and will pay the party for the cannon if he must.

In the event that the party hides, the pirates search for the *Cannon of the Blessed* for two days before abandoning their quest and departing. If the party doesn't have any of the parts of the cannon, then the pirates find them and bring them to Vocini, who assembles them. He will test out its might on the tower before leaving with it.

Yokik Swiftblade

While it's not intended for Yokik to be involved in combat or the story beyond the narrative, players don't always follow the intended plans.

Yokik Swiftblade is a retired hero who owns a castle inland near the border with the nation of giants. She is committed to the stability and health of her nation and is unable to be bribed. She firmly believes that the cannon should be found and returned to the chancellor's control and that Vocini should be put down. She's never encountered Vocini, but has a deep loathing of pirates.

9th level Fighter, STR: 17 (+3), DEX: 16 (+2), CON:16 (+2), INT: 14 (+1), WIS: 9 (0), CHA 15 (+2) AC 0 [19], 60 HP, Att 1x weapon, THAC0 14 [+5], MV 120' (40'), SV D8 W9 P10 B10 S12, ML 12, AL Lawful Good

Items:

- *Ring of the Leader (see Magical Items)*
- *Ring of Protection +2*
- *Cutlass of the Seas (see Magical Items)*
- *Long sword +3*
- *Bow +2, 10 arrows +3, 10 arrows +1*
- *Chainmail +3*
- *4 Potions of Cure Critical Wounds, 2 Potions of Cure Serious Wounds*

Yokik has a keep outside of the city with more than 80 devoted followers of various levels. While mostly warriors, she also has four mages and two priests. Any whom she summons with her *Ring of the Leader* will be armored and armed with at least one minor magical item.

In the city, Yokik usually has 4 Elite Guards with her.

Elite Guards

5th level Fighter, AC 2 [17], HD 5 (20 HP), Att 1x Sword (1d8+2 strength), THAC0 17 [+2], MV 120' (40'), SV D10 W11 P12 B13 S14 (F5), ML 11, AL Lawful Neutral, XP 175

Items:

- Plate mail armor
- Long sword

Magical Items

Here you will find the details for all the new magical items you won't find in your system's rulebooks. These have been drawn from various volumes of *Wondrous & Perilous™ Treasures* or perhaps will appear in a future volume containing enchanting, dangerous, and fun magical items.

Layout and Legend

Each item is laid out in the same style, shown here:

<table>
<tr><td>Item Name</td></tr>
<tr><td>Allowed Groups/Classes – Power Level
Description of the item and summary of its abilities</td></tr>
</table>

Allowed Groups/Classes

Some magical items are limited in what classes or races are allowed, or not allowed, to use them. The chart below groups classes together by type: Divine, Magical, Rogue, and Warrior. If a magical item can only be used by clerics, it'll say Cleric. If it could be used by any class with a divine connection, it'll say Divine.

Depending on the system used, and the perspective of the GM, some classes may fall into one, multiple, or none of these groups.

Name	Classes & Races
Divine	Cleric, Druid, Paladin, Ranger, Bard
Magical	Illusionist, Magic-User, Drow, Duergar, Elf, Gnome, Half-Elf
Rogue	Acrobat, Assassin, Bard, Thief, Halfling, Half-Orc
Spellcaster	Cleric, Drow, Druid, Elf, Gnome, Illusionist, Magic-User
Warrior	Fighter, Knight, Paladin, Ranger, Dwarf, Elf, Half-Elf, Half-Orc, Svirfneblin

The *Divine* group covers the group of classes (and applicable race-as-classes) where the character gains abilities, and/or spells, from a god, deity, demon, nature, or something else considered supernaturally powerful. This covers clerics, paladins, druids, some versions of the bard, as well as some versions of the warlock class that have been back-ported to old school and retro gaming systems.

The *Magical* group covers those who have arcane spell casting abilities or similar abilities such as magic-users, illusionists, gnomes and elves (race-as-class). They are drawing their power from the environment rather than from a divine entity.

Rogue covers those classes that use stealth or thieving skills. They focus on the subtle or clever way of resolving situations.

Spellcaster covers those Magical and Divine who actually can cast spells as opposed to have spell-like abilities. Depending on the system being used, Bards and other classes may be included. Note that if the class allows spell casting at a higher level than the character currently is, then they do not count as a spellcaster for this purpose.

Last, but not least, is *Warrior,* those that focus on fighting skills over the subtle or magical way of resolving things. If a class doesn't fall into another category, it is usually included here.

POWER LEVEL

In order to help the GM know how powerful a magical item is, they are given a rank from low, to medium, to high, to legendary. The higher the rank, the more powerful and potentially disruptive the item can be to lower level adventures.

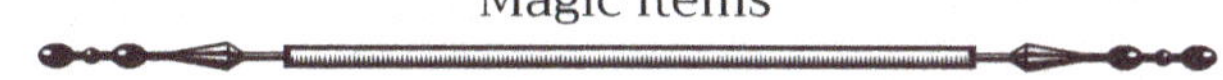

Experience Points and Value of Items

Some GMs and system use the idea of granting an experience point (XP) reward for owning and using a new magical item. The following table provides suggested XP values and the lowest market price for such magical items in gold pieces (GP).

Power Level	Item Type	XP	GP
Low	Potion, Elixirs, Tonics	150	400
	Wands, Staves, Rods	600	3,000
	Rings	800	4,000
	Armor, Garments	300	4,000
	Weapons	800	6,000
	Other & Miscellaneous	400	2,500
Medium	Potion, Elixirs, Tonics	250	900
	Wands, Staves, Rods	1200	8,000
	Rings	1200	9,000
	Armor, Garments	1200	7,000
	Weapons	1400	12,000
	Other & Miscellaneous	800	6,000
High	Potion, Elixirs, Tonics	400	2,000
	Wands, Staves, Rods	2000	20,000
	Rings	1800	15,000
	Armor, Garments	2500	15,000
	Weapons	3500	30,000
	Other & Miscellaneous	2500	25,000
Legendary	Potion, Elixirs, Tonics	750	5,000
	Wands, Staves, Rods	3000	40,000
	Rings	2500	30,000
	Armor, Garments	5000	60,000
	Weapons	7000	90,000
	Other & Miscellaneous	3500	40,000

Items

Arfon's Barrel of Bedlam

*Any – Low [from **Wondrous & Perilous Treasures volume 1**]*

The gnome raced down the deserted streets of the town, his feet sliding from the rains that had only just stopped. Thunderous footsteps were coming, and with them, certain doom.

Spying two wizards arguing behind the Wizard's Guild and a barrel slowly rolling to stop, the gnome managed to get himself over, and into, the barrel without anyone noticing.

The footsteps approached, words were exchanged, and then the moment the gnome feared happened. The barrel was set upright and its lid removed.

He stared at the disappointed faces and was amazed as the lid was put back.

- **Empty is as empty was**. To anyone with normal vision, the barrel appears empty. To those with magical sight, they can sense that it has content but not see what exactly, as if their eyes don't want to focus on it.

- **Roomy**. On the outside, the barrel is 40" tall and has a diameter of 28". On the inside, it is 3' deep with a 3' diameter.

- **Unbreakable.** The barrel is able to withstand an incredible amount of damage (100 HP) without affecting anyone or anything inside rather than rattling it about.

- **Sealed for safe keeping**. The lid is able to be locked from the inside, making it extremely difficult to physically open (like bashing a door, or strength check, with a -1 penalty). It can magically hold 2 hours of air.

Arrows of the Melee Master

Rogue, Warrior – Low

After the death of a close friend, a fletcher known simply as the Melee Master dedicated her life to refining the magic to allow their arrows to weave in and around all obstacles and people, staying true to their intended target. Many would say that she hit the mark.

These arrows are generally available in a +1 and +2 variety.

- **What crowd?** This arrow can be shot safely into melee combat at a target provided that you are able to see the target, at least intermittently. The arrow will weave around creatures and obstacles.

- **Re-covered**. Any target hiding behind some form of cover, other than complete cover, has the level of cover reduced by a quarter. Meaning if they are half covered, it only serves as quarter cover against an *Arrow of the Melee Master*. If the target has quarter cover, they are not covered at all.

- **Missed? Done**. If the arrow misses the target, it immediately plants itself into the ground, ceiling, or otherwise stops instead of continuing on. It does not hit unintended targets.

Boots of Water Walking

Any - Low

These fine boots always seem to be in need of drying out just a bit longer.

- **Water you doing? Just walk**. With these boots on your feet, you can walk on water at will. You can decide when this happens and when this ability is activated, and you will rise up to the surface at a rate of 5 feet per round.

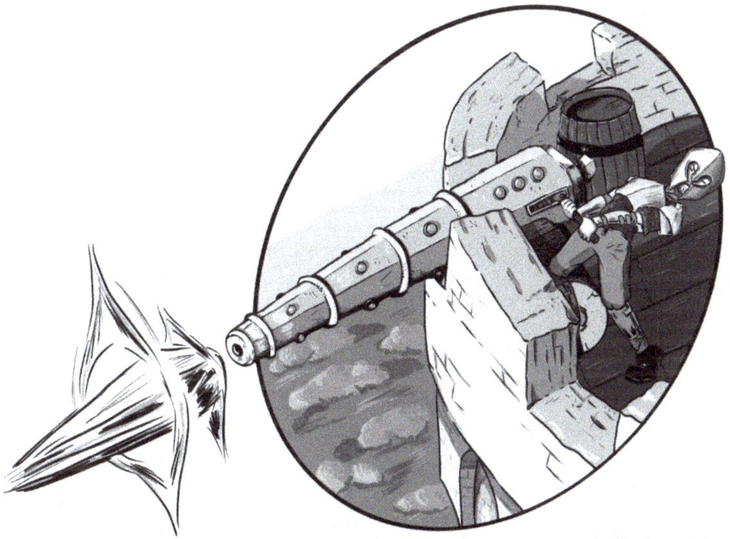

Cannon of the Blessed

*Rogue, Warrior - Legendary [from **Wondrous & Perilous Treasures volume 2**]*

This rather large magical item consists of a culverin and a wooden, wheeled cart that allows it to be moved around, though not easily. Compared to more common ship cannons, it has a longer barrel and looks like it would fire a lighter shot, though it fires magically created ones. Regardless of its

appearance, it's sure to get the attention of the enemy, even if it's only for their final seconds.

- **Reach out and touch someone.** The cannon target opponents up to 1000 feet away (point blank range 100 feet, short range 250 feet, medium range 500 feet, long range 1000 feet) and within a 45-degree arc from the direction it's pointing.

- **Hit'n and hurt'n.** Before firing, you need to spend one round connected to it and concentrating. When it fires, it launches a shimmering, magical ball of blue-flame energy at the target. The target takes 6d6 damage or Save versus Breath Weapon (Dexterity) for half-damage. All those within 10 feet of the target take 4d6 damage or Save versus Breath Weapon (Dexterity) for half-damage. In addition to more damage, a failed saving throw means that they are stunned for one round.

- **Good things take time**. After the cannon has fired, it requires one round of concentration for it to be ready again. If you are attacked and your concentration threatened, the GM can decide if you need to make a Wisdom check.

- **Deafening boom**. Cannons are not subtle or quiet! While the *Cannon of the Blessed* protects those within 5 feet of it from its epic boom, those up to 20 feet away (friend and foe) must Save versus Paralysis (Constitution) or be stunned for one round (-2 to hit, -2 to AC).

- **Limited movement**. While the cannon's frame is on wheels, it cannot be moved more than 20 feet per round without potentially having it fall out of its frame. Lifting the cannon takes a total combined strength of 40.

Cutlass of the Seas

Rogue, Warrior – Medium

This curved-blade short sword is made for those who love fighting on land and the sea.

- **Have at ye.** The cutlass gives +1 to hit and +2 damage on land, and +2 to hit and +3 damage when fighting on or in the water. Its base damage is 1d6+1.

- **Shuffling about.** When holding the cutlass, you can move through water at regular speed rather than being slowed down.

- **Sturdy**. Whenever on water (ship, raft, rocks) all dexterity checks are a bit easier (bonus +1 to the die roll).

Halberd of the Storm

*Warrior – Medium [from **Wondrous & Perilous volume 1**]*

This lengthy weapon has been underestimated many a time, until it led a ship's crew to victory and another time showed a

mad mage that they really should have learned some offensive spells other than lightning.

- **A fine blade**. The halberd has +2 hit and +2 damage. Base damage is 1d10.

- **Charge it**. If the wielder is hit with lightning damage, the halberd absorbs it and can fire it out at opponents the next round (or else it dissipates). The opponent must Save versus Wands (Dex) to avoid damage.

- **Gust of wind**. Instead of attacking, the wielder can issue a strong gust of wind from the halberd. Traveling in a cone, it affects opponents up to 60' away and requires them to save versus spells (Wis) or be knocked back and off their feet. This can be used up to 3x day.

- **What rain?** The wielder is able to ignore any effects of storms such as limited vision and slippery surfaces.

- **Light the way**. The halberd is able to light up an area up to 30' radius at will.

Hilt of the Discerning

*Rogue, Warrior – Low [from **Wondrous & Perilous volume 1**]*

The hilt is sized for a long sword, and in place of where a blade would go is a piece of ebony stone. When the wielder holds the hilt in one hand and a sword in another, and brings them together, the Hilt of the Discerning turns the other to ash and attaches itself to the blade. Then, with a whispered magical word, the blade retracts into the hilt, leaving only the ebony stone.

- **Choice is everything**. The hilt can store three swords inside itself, without changing the weight of the hilt. Each blade is able to be called forth instantly with a magic word. A blade can be released at any time and drops to the ground, though without a hilt.

Potion of Graceful Step

Any – Low

"I swear, the more he drinks, the better he seems to get."

"Don't let him hear you say that."

This potion looks like a bottle of alcohol, often with a golden or crimson tint to it. The effects, however, are notably different.

- **Watch me now.** After consuming you, you have +2 to your dexterity (max 20) for 1 hour.

Potion of Mighty Strength

Any - Low

Having a translucent green appearance, with chunks in it, this potion tastes terrible but provides benefits that are well worth it.

- **Flex.** Upon drinking the whole potion, you have +2 to your strength (max 20) for 1 hour.

Ring of Encounters

Any - Low

"Hey, Alfonsa. Is that yet another group of goblins ahead?"

"It does appear so, yes."

"We're lost in the middle of a forest, but we still seem to be able to find someone who wants a piece of us every hour or so."

"It does appear that way."

"Any idea why?"

Alfonsa looked at her ring, playing with it, thinking hard for a minute. Sighing, she shrugged. "I don't know. Perhaps it's just bad luck."

- **Attention getter.** When worn, this ring looks enchanting to you, makes you feel it looks good on you. Its only power to increase the chances of a random encounter by +2 or by 30% (depending on the tables being used, to be decided upon by the GM).

Ring of Thudisi

*Any - Medium [from **Wondrous & Perilous Volume 1**]*

Everyone stared over the cliff in horror and disbelief as the impulsive warrior plunged hundreds of feet and landed with an audible thump. "He didn't fall like a feather."

To their surprise, he stood up, offered a wave, and was off. What in the world?

- **Sucking it up like a buttercup.** The wearer can fall up to 300' without taking any damage. For greater falls, subtract 300' from the total distance and reduce damage by half.

- **Hero-ish landing.** Upon landing, the wearer rolls a d8 on the following chart (add their dexterity bonus or penalty to their roll).

Ring of the Arborist

Any - Medium

Covered with living leaves and a thin roots, this ring has a connection to the natural world. It provides these abilities:

- **Protection.** You have +1 bonus to AC against plants and plant-based creatures.

- **Immunity**. When hit with a speciality from a plants or plant-based creature, you have a 2-in-6 chance of being immune to the effect that round.

- **Climb.** You are able to climb trees and vines at a normal rate of climbing, even if wet.

- **Unimpeded**. You are able to move through thick brush and forest as without penalty.

Ring of the Leader

Warrior - Medium

"Surrender! We have you outnumbered," yelled the bandit king. "Foolish of you to have waltzed right into our lair alone."

"Alone you say?" The leader rubbed the ring on their finger and instantly the tables were turned.

A prize for any leader who has built a following, this ring is creates a connection back to the leader's stronghold and allows them to summon their followers.

- **Reinforcements**. If you have a following and stronghold, you are able to teleport up to 12 followers to your aid provided you are within 500 miles. They arrive aware of your situation and ready to render aid. This can be used once per day.

- **Return.** You are able to return up to 12 followers back to your stronghold provided you are within 500 miles. You are only able to send them back with up to 100 lbs beyond what they arrived with when summoned, or if not summoned, what they would have been wearing and holding. This can be used once per day.

- **Retreat.** Sometimes, there is no path forward. Once per day, you are able to teleport back to a place you have marked in your stronghold provided the stronghold is within 500 miles and you are at least 5 miles away.

Scroll Case of Power

Magical - Medium

Ornately crafted and speckled with gem dust, this case is able to fit a single scroll which after a full day, is more powerful than it was.

- **Magical protection.** Any scroll placed in the case is free from harm unless anti-magic is used.

- **Power boost.** If the stored scroll does damage, then after a full day it does an additional d8 and saving throws against it are at a -1 penalty. If the stored scroll doesn't do damage, then it's duration is increased by 20% and saving throws against it are at a -1 penalty.

Short Sword of the Flame

Rogue, Warrior - High

This sword is made of a fine steel. Its hilt is encased a strange, white stone, and the blade has a ruby red insert that goes from the hilt to the tip of the its blade.

- **Light the way**. You are able to make the sword burst into an illuminating flame at will. This can light up an area up to 30 feet around you. The flame works like a torch, meaning it can be used to set things on fire and can be blown out with a strong gust of wind, or if dosed in waterver. If blown out, it takes 1d4 rounds to reignite.

- **Well suited for battle**. The blade provides you a +2 to hit and +2 damage, as well as 1d6 additional fire damage against opponents affected by fire or heat.

- **Particularly well suited for some**. The blade has higher bonuses to hit and damage against certain creatures: +3 vs ice and cold creatures, as well as trolls and tree-folk.

- **Protect my soul and being**. The blade gives you a +1 on saving throws versus magical and natural fire.

Shrinking Spear of Wounding

Warrior - Medium

Some weapons are designed to draw attention, to be spectacles to behold and then there are those like the *Shrinking Spear of Wounding*. The spear appears remarkably well made, but ordinary, with no details or anything distinctive, save for a few glyphs on the blade.

- **Out of sight**. When held, and the command word uttered, the spear is able to shrink down to four inches or back to full size.

- **Well balanced**. The spear gives you a +2 to hit and +3 damage when used in melee or thrown.

- **Wounding**. Every wound by the spear that caused at least 1 point of damage will continue to cause 1 point of damage until the target is healed.

Staff of Submission

Magical - Medium

This staff usually has a sapphire or ruby head and is about two feet long. It is regal in appearance and has a hearty weight to it.

- **By my command**. You are able to use charm up to 2d4 creatures of 2 hit dice or less, similar to the spell *Charm Monster*. This lasts for up to 8 hours and can be used up to 3x per day.

- **Negate charm**. You are able to dispel magical charm on any creature by touching them with the end of the staff.

Staff of Travel

Magical - Medium

This wooden staff is decorated with pictures of different landscapes, buildings, and people.

- **A bridge to new opportunities**. Three times per day, the staff can cast a version of *Dimension Door* that lasts up to 5 minutes (or until dispelled). One end of the portal must be created within 10 feet of you as you wield the staff, note that it does not move if you do.

- **No go zone.** Once per day, when wielding the staff, you can create a zone (90-foot radius) around you that is unable to be magically travelled into. This blocks any magical teleportation, dimension doors, etc. other than ones created by the staff itself. Any attempts to use travel magic will randomly send the person somewhere within a 1 mile radius.

Spyglass of the Pathfinder

*Any - Low [from **Wondrous & Perilous Treasures volume 2**]*

There are many tales of lost travelers who miraculously found their way and those who could find a ring lost in a desert. This spyglass grants its wielder more than superior vision.

- **Clear view**. The spyglass allows you to see clearly for up to a 1 mile away ignoring fog, snow, and rain.

- **Finders keepers**. If you have a clear idea of what you are looking for, for example you have a piece of cloth of a missing person, or have been given a detailed description of an item (GM's decision), the spyglass will act as a *Locate Object* spell targeting it. If you are outside, it will point you in the right direction if the target is within 5 miles. If indoors or underground, it will point in the correct direction if the target is within 500 feet. This can be used up to three times per day and lasts for 1 hour.

Toxin of the Ghoul

Any - Medium - Twisted (from Wondrous & Perilous Treasures volume 1)

"Gah! What did you do to me? That tasted like acid. I swear it's ripping the life right out of me." The paladin stumbled about, clutching at his chest. His face went grey momentarily.

The rogue snatched the flask out of the paladin's limp hand and held it up to the light. "There it is. The green that has bled gives reward to the red." He took a swig from the potion. Rolling his shoulders and cracking his neck, he patted the weary paladin on the shoulder. "Ah, I needed that."

This elixir's real magic is in the flask more than the liquid, for whatever liquid is put into it will be twisted after a month. Once twisted, the liquid will be a green mixture, which if consumed, pulls life out. This will then make the mixture change to a crimson red. The next consumer will be given that life.

- **To the first, the pain**. If you drink the green liquid, you receive up to 2d6 damage. The green liquid always leaves its drinker with a minimum of 1 HP. If the rolled damage is more than the drinker has, then the actual difference infuses the potion instead of the rolled damage. It also cannot be used to bring someone up to 1 HP. Drinking the green liquid causes the flask to refill with a dark red liquid.

- **To the second, the gain**. However many hit points were taken by the first drink, you will gain that amount minus 1 HP. For example: if the first person lost 6 HP, then the second person heals 5 HP. After drinking the red liquid, the flask refills with dark green resetting the cycle. It can be used up to once per day.

Vial of Potent Healing

Any - Medium

Often found as a shimmering aquamarine goop in a gold vial, the contents smell bad and taste worse. However, the sludge inside provides a one-time dose of significant healing:

- **Heal**. Restore 3d6 hit points upon drinking the contents.

- **Cleaned up**. You are cured of any poison or disease you have.

- **Revitalized**. If any of your stats (strength, dexterity, etc) have been diminished due to creature ability, poison, or disease, they start being restored at the rate of +1 to one stat, per round, for 1d6 rounds. The stat is your choice.

Player Map - Outdoors - West

Player Map - Outdoors - East

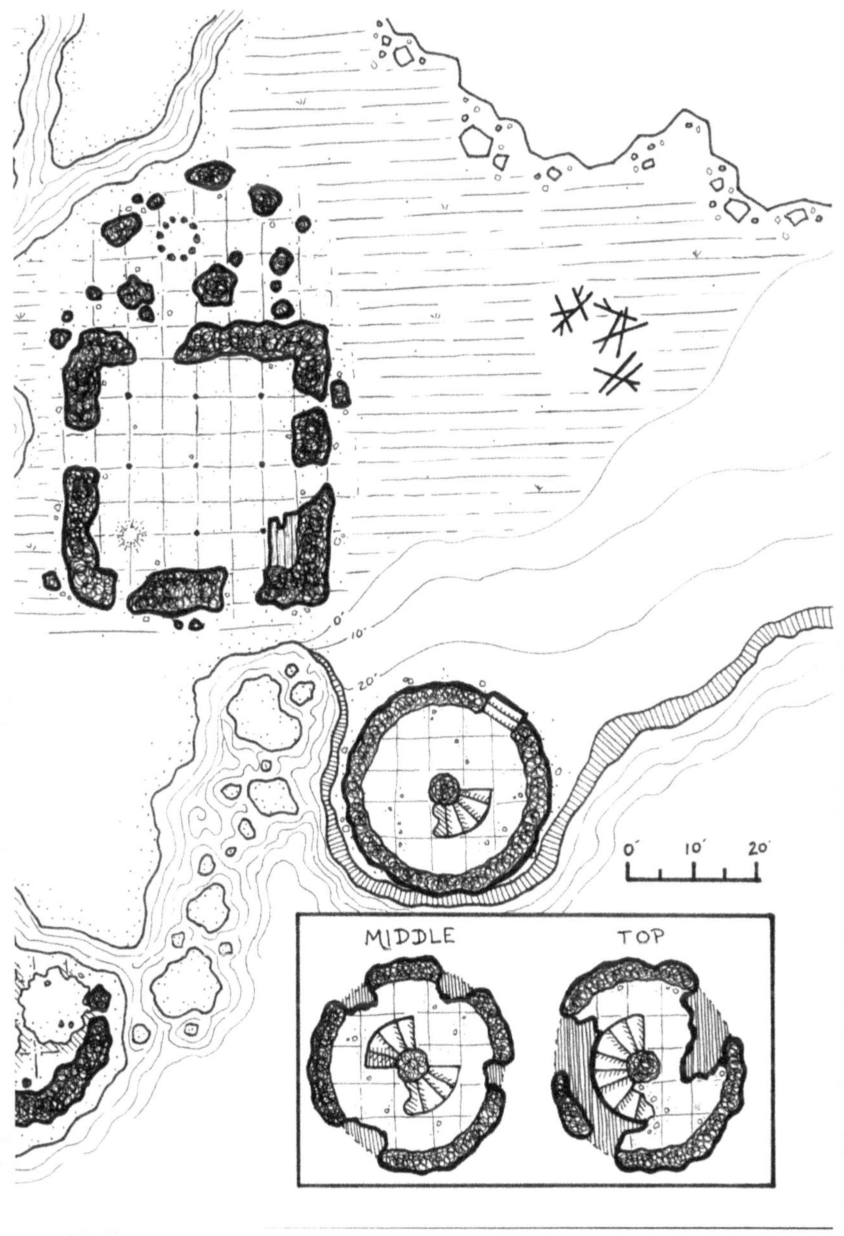

Player Map - Underground

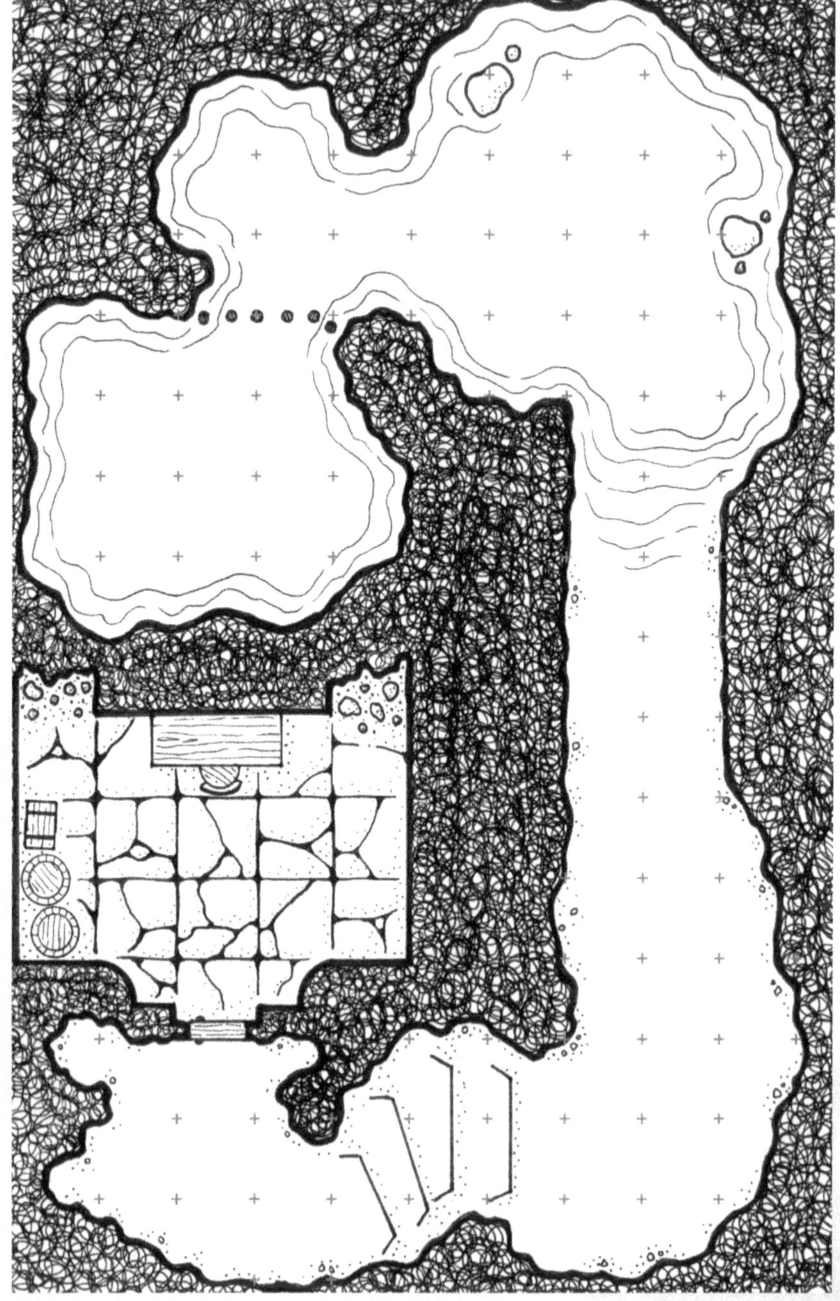

More by Adam Dreece

Over 110 new magical items to bring
trust issues and fun to your table.
Includes magical garments, assistive
magical items, and more.

Discover more at AdamDreece.com

Bring new life to your campaigns

More than 120 new magical items to thrill and chill for your campaign. Among other types of magical items, this volume includes furniture and items for animals.

ADVENTURE AWAITS!

Whether diving into an ancient crypt to stop an evil goblin sorcerer, or wading through a haunted swamp in search of a legendary cannon, discover our growing catalog of great adventures.

Coming Soon

Wondrous & Perilous Tales #1

A collection of fantasy short stories with playable material for your own campaigns.

Coming to Kickstarter.

More Adventures!

Stay tuned for more W&P Adventures, from temples and dungeons to castles and lairs.

Treasures - Volume 3!!

What more can lurk in the imagination of Adam Dreece? Plenty. Another volume of carefully crafted magical items is on its way! This time, with magical foods and herbs.

Coming to Kickstarter.

Don't miss out.

Join the newsletter.

AdamDreece.com

BOOKS BY ADAM DREECE

Final Word

Stay up to date with what's happening, what's going to happen, or say hi. Here's where you can find me:

- Bluesky @adamdreece.bsky.social
- Facebook /AdamDreeceAuthor
- Instagram @AdamDreece
- TikTok @AdamDreece
- Email: adam@adamdreece.com

You can also join my newsletter: adamdreece.com/newsletter